W9-BUB-852

# THE RAILWAY MURDERS

Also by Jonathan Goodman

*The Pleasures of Murder*
*The Stabbing of George Harry Storrs*

# THE RAILWAY MURDERS

*Edited by*

*Jonathan Goodman*

ALLISON & BUSBY

LONDON

First published 1984
by Allison & Busby Limited
6a Noel Street, London W1V 3RB, England

British Library Cataloguing in Publication Data:

The Railway murders.
  1. Murder—England—History    2. Crimes
  aboard trains—England—History
  I. Goodman, Jonathan
  364.1'523'0942     HV6535.G5E5

ISBN 0-85031-599-9

Photoset in 11/12pt Janson by
Derek Doyle & Associates, Mold, Clwyd
and printed in Great Britain by
Billings & Sons Ltd, Worcester

# Contents

# Points
## *of*
## *Departure*

Jonathan Goodman

READING BETWEEN the lines of crime fiction, one gathers that writers of that genre are, as often as not, railway enthusiasts. Patricia Highsmith arranged for strangers to meet on a train, Ethel Lina White caused a lady to vanish on one, Agatha Christie schemed a murder on the Orient Express, James M. Cain made a double-indemnity insurance fiddle seem, to the defrauders, as simple as falling off an observation platform; Freeman Wills Crofts, a railway engineer till he took early retirement so as to devote his time to writing, made play with trains in most of his novels.

Writers of crime fiction have a choice of several reasons (loco-motives, one supposes) for taking to the railway: an enclosed setting — ideal for a variation on the Locked-Room Mystery — but a constantly changing view; an impression of speed that may give an impression of pace; the opportunity to take a tale across county or state borders, even national frontiers, disembarking dead passengers and welcoming new and live ones aboard along the permanent way; the Mussoliniesque precision of fictional timetables, handy for establishing time of death and for checking alibis; the democracy of rail-travel — for a train, like the Ritz, is open to everyone, first- and second-class citizens alike.

And so story-tellers have given railways a bad name; have made trains seem dangerous things to travel in; may even have increased customer-resistance to campaigns by British Rail and Amtrak, aimed at boosting sales of return-tickets....

...Unfairly, because statistics indicate that a person boarding a train that is not a football-special is more likely to reach his destination unmurdered, not even molested, than if he had chosen some form of transport other than a bullet-proof, bomb-resistant, self-catering, oxygen-carrying automobile fitted with a carbon-monoxide-measuring gauge and driven by a nun who, if she were permitted the luxury of pride, would be proud of her membership of the Institute of Advanced Motorists.

This book contains accounts by divers authors of ten real "railway murders", three of which are so called because of post-mortem happenings: the fatal acts having been committed away from railway property, the murderers used rail facilities in aid of tidying up. The ten are not the whole tally of British "railway murders" since the first locomotive trundled between Stockton and Darlington in 1825. None of the rest, so it seems to me, warrants more than a few recollective words.

I suppose the conspicuous absentee-victim is Florence Nightingale Shore. Yes, a nurse. On 12 January 1920, she set off from London towards Hastings, intending to stay a few days with friends at the St Leonards addendum to the seaside resort; but before the train stopped at Polegate, north of Eastbourne, was battered about the head. In his good reference-book *A Companion to Murder*, E. Spencer Shew explains that when some platelayers got into the compartment at Polegate,

> they noticed a woman sitting in the corner, but paid her no particular attention, and it was not until some little time afterwards that one of the more observant among them was struck by the peculiar posture in which she was sitting — as if she were about to slide off the seat on to the floor. Then he noticed that there was blood on her face and more blood on the magazine lying open on her lap; glass from her broken spectacles was scattered on the floor. At Bexley [*sic*: Bexhill], Miss Shore, still conscious but unable to speak or to move, was taken from the train to East Sussex Hospital, where she died four days later in a coma induced by a fractured skull and injury to the brain; it was considered that her injuries could have been caused by blows from the butt-end of a revolver. From that day to this nothing has transpired to disturb or amplify the verdict of the coroner's jury: "Wilful murder by a person or persons unknown."

Mr Shew's book was published in 1960, but his comment on the verdict still applies. If, like me, you are as intrigued by the bric-à-brac of murder cases as by the criminal acts and evidences of the crimes, you will wonder what magazine it was that Nurse Shore did not finish reading. However, that detail, if discoverable, would not justify the elongation of the incident into an essay.

Another unsolved crime — the murder, likewise with a blunt instrument, of a barmaid named Elizabeth Camp in a second-class compartment of a Waterloo-bound train that departed Feltham, a few miles west of London, at 8.25 on the evening of 11 February 1897 — might well have been solved, and would even more probably have become worthy of an account, had the railway police not kept the crime to themselves, leaving Scotland Yard to learn of it by chance and so long after the event that clues had either gone cold or been crunched under railway policemen's boots. As it is, there is no apparent story but just three picturesque facts that deserve to be noted, one being that Miss Camp's place of employment was called the Good Intent (no decent novelist would allow that sort of irony past the first draft); another being that the murder weapon, found on the side of the line, bloodstained and with hair clinging to it, was a pestle; the third being that, on the day of the funeral, hawkers did a brisk trade in moist-from-the-press memorial cards:

| |
|---|
| Sacred to the memory of<br>Elizabeth Annie Camp,<br>aged 33,<br>who was brutally murdered on February 11,<br>between Hounslow and Waterloo Station<br>on the London and South Western Railway<br>Rest in Peace. |

Although most acknowledgements are made, and most sources identified, elsewhere in this book, I should like to

11

separate my thanks to Colin Wilson and Pat Pitman, who suggested that I might like to couple an appendix to their *Encyclopaedia of Murder* (published in 1961) with the account of the Dickman case; and to my friend James Hodge, last general editor of William Hodge and Company's "Notable British Trials", who has reason to be irritated at the pillaging of that splendid series of volumes but who raised no objection to my using parts of the introductions to both *Trial of John Alexander Dickman* (first published in 1914; revised edition, 1926) and *Trial of Franz Muller* (published in 1911).

It pleases me that the account of the first British "railway murder" is by H. B. Irving, the actor and author who in 1903 invited fellow connoisseurs of crime to a dinner, thus founding Our Society, otherwise known as the "Crimes Club", and that the contribution on the Brighton trunk cases is a version of a paper read to members of that society and their guests three-quarters of a century later. Not because of the link, and not only because His Honour Judge Henry Elam has been secretary of Our Society since 1952, I dedicate this book to him.

JONATHAN GOODMAN

# The First
# Railway Murder

## H.B. Irving

ON THE night of Saturday, 9 July 1864, a suburban train on the North London Railway left Fenchurch Street station for Chalk Farm at 9.50. It left the next station, Bow, at 10.1; Hackney Wick or Victoria Park, at 10.5; and arrived at Hackney about six minutes later. At the last station two bank clerks, who had taken tickets for Highbury, opened the door of a compartment of a first-class carriage. The carriage was empty. The two men got in and sat down. They had hardly done so when one called the other's attention to some blood on his hand. They alighted immediately from the carriage, and called the guard of the train. He examined the compartment, and discovered stains of blood on the cushions of the seat which backed to the engine on the left-hand side of the train going from London. There was blood on the glass by the cushion, some marks of blood on the cushion opposite, and on the offside handle of the carriage door. In the carriage the guard found a hat, stick, and bag. These he took out, the carriage was locked up, taken to Chalk Farm station, and later brought back to Bow.

About twenty minutes past ten on the same night the driver of a train of empty carriages from Hackney Wick to Fenchurch Street noticed a dark object lying on the six-foot way between the Hackney Wick and Bow stations. He stopped the train, alighted from the engine, and found that the dark object was the body of a man. He was lying on his back between the up and down lines, his feet towards London and his head towards Hackney, at a spot about two-thirds of the distance — 1 mile 414 yards — between Bow and Hackney stations. The body was taken to a neighbouring public-house, and a doctor summoned. He found that the unfortunate man was alive, but completely unconscious, that his skull had been fractured, and several wounds inflicted on his head, presumably by some blunt instrument, while there were a number of jagged wounds near the left ear.

The victim of this apparently atrocious assault was soon identified as Mr Thomas Briggs, chief clerk in the bank of Messrs Robarts & Co., of Lombard Street. Mr Briggs remained unconscious until late the following night, when he expired. At the time of his death he was close on seventy years of age, a gentleman greatly trusted and respected by his employers, and held in high esteem by a large circle of friends. He resided at Victoria Park, and was a frequent traveller between Fenchurch Street and Hackney Wick, or Victoria Park, station. On the evening of 9 July Mr Briggs had dined with some relations, and left their house at Peckham, carrying a black bag and a walking-stick, about half-past eight. He had walked from there to the Old Kent Road, where he had taken an omnibus to King William Street for the purpose of getting to Fenchurch Street station. At Fenchurch Street Mr Briggs was seen and spoken to by the ticket collector, who knew him well, as he passed through with his ticket to enter the 9.50 train for Hackney Wick. From that moment Mr Briggs had been seen by no one until he was found insensible on the railway.

In the bloodstained carriage a bag, a stick, and a hat had been found. The bag and stick were both recognized as having belonged to Mr Briggs, and been in his possession when he quitted his friend's house, but the hat was not his. The tall hat worn by Mr Briggs had disappeared; the hat found in the carriage was a black beaver hat, but lower in the crown than the ordinary high hat such as Mr Briggs was in the habit of wearing. Inside the hat was the name of the maker, "Mr J. H. Walker, 49 Crawford Street, Marylebone".

This hat seemed to be the only possible clue to the identity of the assailant, for that Mr Briggs had been the victim of a foul murder there could be no reasonable doubt. No weapon capable of inflicting the injuries on the head of the murdered man had been found; but it was thought possible, though by no means certain, that, wielded by a powerful arm, these might have been inflicted by Mr Briggs's walking-stick, which was large, heavy and stained with blood. From the appearance of the compartment it seemed likely that Mr Briggs had been attacked while dozing, with his head against the corner of the carriage. Though nearly seventy years of age, he was described as a stout, stalwart man, who, had he been fully alert, would no doubt have made a desperate resistance. Whether he had been thrown on the line by his assailant or had struggled and fallen from the carriage in his endeavour to escape was a matter of conjecture, though here, again, the probability was that he had been flung on the line. Robbery had been the motive of the crime; though some £5 in money had been left in the pockets of the murdered man, his gold watch and chain and gold eye-glasses were missing, only the gold fastening of the watch-chain being left attached to the waistcoat.

Great public interest and indignation were aroused by the crime. It was the first murder on an English railway, of a character very alarming to a public less inured to such crimes than we are to-day. The government and Messrs Robarts' Bank offered each a reward of £100 for the discovery of the murderer, and these offers were followed shortly after by another £100 from the North London Railway. The first clue to the identity of the murderer was furnished by a jeweller of the not inappropriate name of Death. He stated that on the morning of Monday, 11 July, a man of about thirty years of age, of sallow complexion and thin in feature, apparently a German, but speaking good English, had called at his shop in Cheapside, and had exchanged for a gold chain and a ring to the total value of £3 10s., a gold albert chain, which Death recognized from the published description as the chain worn by Mr Briggs on the night of his murder. He described the man as having been perfectly self-possessed during the quarter of an hour he was in his shop, but said that he placed himself all the time in such a position as not to be exposed to a full view.

For another six days rumour was busy and speculation rife as to the nature of the crime and the identity of the murderer. Some suggested that the crime had been an act of revenge on the part of an employee of Messrs Robarts' Bank whom Mr Briggs had, in the course of his duty, seen fit to discharge. But on 18 July a cabman named Jonathan Matthews made a statement to the police, which seemed to indicate clearly the identity of the perpetrator of the crime. Matthews, who appears to have been a man of very moderate intelligence, and certainly no great reader, had, according to his own account, heard nothing of the murder that was agitating all London, until talking of the crime with a man on the cab rank, his attention was arrested by the name of the jeweller Death. He then recollected that he had seen in his own house a few days previously a jeweller's cardboard box bearing the rather singular name of Death. This box had been given to his little girl by a young German of the name of Franz Müller. Müller had been at one time engaged to one of Matthews's daughters, but, owing to his unreasonable jealousy, the engagement had been broken off.

Müller was a native of Saxe-Weimar, twenty-five years of age. Apprenticed as a gunsmith in his native country, he had come over to England about two years before the murder of Mr Briggs. Failing to get work as a gunsmith, he had turned tailor, and had been working up to 2 July in the employment of a Mr Hodgkinson. Müller was not satisfied, however, with the conditions of work in England, and had declared his intention of going away to seek his fortune in America. In accordance with this intention he had left England on Friday, 15 July, by the sailing ship *Victoria*, bound from the London Docks for New York.

The cabman Matthews supplied the police with another link in the chain of evidence against Müller. He identified the hat found in the railway carriage as a hat which he had himself purchased for Müller at the shop of a Mr Walker in Crawford Street, Marylebone. He was able to supply the police with a photograph of Müller, and the address of the house in which Müller had been lodging immediately before his departure for America. The photograph was shown to Death, who at once identified it as that of the man who on Monday, 11 July, had visited his shop and exchanged Mr Briggs's gold chain for another.

Müller had been lodging last with a Mr and Mrs Blyth at

18

*Franz Muller. (By kind permission of Madame Tussaud & Sons).*

16 Park Terrace, Bow, so that he had been in the habit of travelling on the same railway line, to and from Fenchurch Street, as the late Mr Briggs. Mrs Blyth gave her lodger an excellent character. "He was," she said, "a quiet, well-behaved, inoffensive young man, of a humane and affectionate disposition." She stated that on Saturday, 9 July, the day of the murder, Müller had gone out as usual in the morning, but had not returned home when she and her husband went to bed at eleven o'clock. On the following day, Sunday, she said that he had been in the best of spirits, laughing, chatting, and enjoying his meals. On the Monday evening Müller had shown Mrs Blyth the gold chain which he had got from Death in exchange for that taken from Mr Briggs. Since his departure for America Mrs Blyth had received a letter from Müller, posted from Worthing. It ran as follows:

On the sea, July 16th, in the morning. Dear friends, I am glad to confess that I cannot have a better time as I have, for the sun shines nice and the wind blows fair as it is at present moment, everything will go well. I cannot write any more

19

only I have no postage, you will be so kind as to take that letter in.

Besides this letter, Mrs Blyth showed the police a hatbox which Müller had brought with him when he first came to lodge at her house. It bore on it the name of Walker, Crawford Street, Marylebone, the name of the shop from which Matthews had stated that he had bought the hat for Müller.

The police lost no time in getting on the track of the young German tailor. Matthews made his statement at ten o'clock on the night of 18 July. At half-past six the following morning the officers called on Mrs Blyth, and the same night Inspector Tanner and Detective-Sergeant Clarke, taking with them the jeweller Death, the cabman Matthews, and a warrant granted by Mr Henry, chief magistrate at Bow Street, for Müller's arrest, left Euston station for Liverpool. They sailed from there for New York on Tuesday, 20 July, by the New York and Philadelphia Company's steamship *City of Manchester*. The steamer was timed to arrive at New York some two or three weeks before the sailing ship that was carrying Müller. The proceedings of the police in this case bear some resemblance to those employed in the capture of Crippen, save that in 1864 there was no wireless telegraphy to assure the police officers that the *Victoria* had their man on board. Inspector Tanner and his companions reached New York on 5 August. They had to wait twenty days before the *Victoria* came into port. By that time New York had become as excited as London over the expected arrival of Müller, and in their excitement some foolish persons all but prevented the police from taking Müller alive. As the *Victoria* was waiting in harbour for the pilot boat containing the officers to come out to her, a party of excursionists passing near the vessel shouted out, "How are you, Müller the murderer?" Fortunately Müller, who was on deck, did not hear them. Had he done so, he might have evaded capture by timely suicide. As soon as the officers came on board, the captain ordered all the steerage passengers aft for medical examination. Müller was called into the cabin. He was charged with the murder of Mr Briggs on the North

London Railway on the night of 9 July. He turned very pale, but said that he had never been on that line. His keys were taken from him, his box searched, and in it were found the watch and what was believed to be the hat of the late Mr Briggs. Müller said that they were both his property; that he had had the watch for two years and the hat for about twelve months.

Müller on landing in New York was an object of great interest to the public. He is described as short, with light hair and "small grey, inexpressible eyes". He had behaved fairly well on the voyage out, but had got into trouble once or twice on account of his overbearing manner. On one occasion he received a black eye for calling a fellow-passenger a liar and a robber. He had no money with him, but tried to raise some by offering to eat 5lbs of German sausage. He failed in this laudable endeavour, and was compelled to stand porter all round, a penalty he could only fulfil by parting with two of his shirts.

On 26 August extradition proceedings were commenced before Commissioner Newton, and concluded the following day. Death, Matthews, and the police officers gave evidence. Müller was represented by a Mr Chauncey Schaffer. In addressing the Commissioner on behalf of his client, Mr Schaffer made no reference to the charge against him. He indulged in a harangue in the true "Jefferson Brick" vein, punctuated by loud applause, in which he denounced the British for their flagrant iniquity in regard to the ship *Alabama*, which had been destroyed in the previous June, and said that by our own treachery and gross misconduct we had made any Extradition Treaty a dead letter. The Commissioner, while tactfully complimenting Mr Schaffer on his address, did not yield to his singular arguments. He granted Müller's extradition, and on 3 September Müller and his captors left for England on the steamship *Etna* of the Inman Line.

In England Müller's arrival was no less eagerly awaited than that of Dr Crippen. The dramatic flight and capture of the young German had given the case a degree of interest which it had failed to awaken at the outset. Even *The Times* accorded large headings to the news of Müller which was coming from America. For the moment the news of Müller seemed almost to eclipse in importance that of the Civil War then raging in the United States beween North and South. It was pointed out by some English newspapers that had Müller possessed $3000 or $4000 at the time of his arrest in New York, he might have procured bail from the Commissioner, and been quietly spirited away into the ranks of the Federal Army. According to these newspapers, American law at this time allowed bail to all accused persons, whatever the nature of their offence. But Müller was penniless and without friends. There was to be no military career for him — he was not to lose his life upon the field of battle.

During his absence from England the question of Müller's guilt had been widely discussed. The weight of the evidence against him, especially that of the cabman Matthews, had been made a subject of newspaper correspondence. To such lengths had this improper discussion been carried that the *Daily Telegraph* published a leading article warning the public against forming a premature judgement of the case against Müller. To help him to secure the best assistance at his trial the German Legal Protection Society announced that they had undertaken his defence.

The *Etna* arrived at Queenstown on the evening of 15 September. A representative of the *Daily Telegraph* visited Müller in his cabin, and found him quiet and cheerful. On his undertaking, willingly given, that he would cause no trouble, the officers had dispensed with the use of handcuffs. The young man seemed greatly interested in a shoal of porpoises, and pointed out some cows on the Irish coast which could only have been described by a man with extremely good sight. Müller was reading *David Copperfield*. He had been given *Pickwick* at the commencement of the voyage, and had enjoyed the book so well, especially the account of the trial of Bardell *v.* Pickwick, that he had asked for another work by the same author. His conduct during the voyage had been exemplary; he alluded with evident pleasure to the fact that as a prisoner on the *Etna* he was enjoying much better food than had been

supplied to the steerage passengers on the *Victoria*.
Liverpool was reached on the night of Friday, the 16th.
There a strange incident occurred. A well-dressed and
apparently gentlemanly person walked into the room where
Müller was waiting, and, going up to him, said, "And you are
Franz Müller. Well, I am glad to see you and shake hands with
you. Do you think you will be able to prove your innocence?"
To which Müller replied "I do." "You know, Müller," said
the gentleman in a loud voice, "this is a very serious charge."
Here one of the detectives interposed and told the man to
leave the room, which he did, but with some reluctance. His
fatuous conduct was made the theme of a stinging rebuke in
*Punch*, under the heading of "An Awful Snob at Liverpool".
At nine o'clock on the Saturday morning Müller left for
London, reaching Euston at a quarter to three. A large crowd
greeted him with hoots and groans. He was taken at once to
Bow Street, and charged, after which he was removed to
Holloway Prison.

On the following Monday the magisterial hearing
commenced at the Bow Street Police Court before Mr
Flowers. Mr Hardinge Giffard — later Lord Halsbury —
appeared to prosecute for the Crown, and Müller was
defended by a well-known solicitor, Mr Thomas Beard, who
had been instructed by the German Legal Protection Society.
The evidence, which was substantially that given afterwards at
the trial, need not be recapitulated here. One important new
piece of evidence was that of a hatter, Dan Digance, and his
assistant, who had been in the habit of making Mr Briggs's
hats. They declared that the hat found in Müller's box was a
hat made by them; that it had been cut down an inch and a
half and sewn together again, but not in such a way as a hatter
would have done it; a hatter, they said, would have used gum.
They stated that it was their custom to write the name of the
customer for whom the hat had been made on the band of the
hat inside the lining. This part of the hat had been cut away
from the hat found in Müller's box. Müller was remanded
until Monday, 26 September. That day, at eight o'clock in the
morning, he attended the last sitting of the coroner's inquest

at the Hackney Town Hall, when the jury returned a verdict of wilful murder against him. From Hackney he was taken to Bow Street at eleven o'clock, and at the end of the day's hearing Mr Flowers committed him for trial at the Central Criminal Court. No evidence was called on behalf of the prisoner. The magistrate asked Müller if he had anything to say. He answered, "No, sir, I have nothing to say now." Throughout the proceedings Müller had appeared cool and collected, only betraying anger on one occasion during the evidence of Matthews, the cabman.

The Sessions at the Central Criminal Court opened on Monday, 24 October, when the Recorder, Mr Russell Gurney, advised the jury to bring in a true bill against Franz Müller. This they returned on the following Wednesday, and on the next day, Thursday, the 27th, Müller was put upon his trial. The presiding judges were the Lord Chief Baron, Sir Frederick Pollock, and his son-in-law, Mr Baron Martin — two of the most distinguished judges on the bench. In these more leisurely days a law officer of the Crown did not disdain to conduct the prosecution in a sensational trial for murder. On this occasion Sir Robert Collier, Solicitor-General, led for the Crown with a very strong team of assistants at his back. First and foremost among them was Serjeant Ballantine, one of the most popular advocates of the day, noted more particularly for his great skill as a cross-examiner. His juniors were Mr Hardinge Giffard, Mr Hannen, and Mr Beasley.

Serjeant Parry led for the defence. His tact and skill as a verdict getter, his great powers of persuasion with a jury, made Parry one of the most popular and successful advocates of his time, whilst his kind and genial nature had rendered him no less popular as a man. Mr Metcalfe and Mr Besley were his juniors.

Needless to say, the Court was crowded throughout the trial. The Lord Mayor Lawrence accompanied the judges on the bench. Müller is described as pale and anxious, following the proceedings closely and communicating frequently with his solicitor, Mr Beard. Sir Robert Collier opened the case for the Crown in a short and business-like speech. He suggested

that Mr Briggs had been attacked while dozing in the corner
of the carriage, and that the weapon with which the deed had
been done had undoubtedly been Mr Briggs's walking-stick
— "a formidable weapon, large, heavy, with a handle at one
end". As motive for the crime the Solicitor-General suggested
a sudden desire that had come over the murderer to possess
the gold watch and chain which stood out conspicuously on
the waistcoat of his victim. He attached great importance to
the hat found in the railway carriage — "If you discover with
certainty," he said, "the person who wore that hat on that
night, you will have the murderer, and the case is proved
almost as clearly against him as if he was seen to do it." He
showed how by his dealings with pawnbrokers and others,
commencing from the exchange of Mr Briggs's watch-chain
with Death, the prisoner had become possessed of about £4
5s. in cash with which, on the Wednesday following the
murder, he had bought his passage to America. He dealt with
the evidence as regards the two hats — the one found in the
carriage, which he would prove to have belonged to Müller,
and the other found in Müller's box in New York, which he
would prove to have belonged to Mr Briggs. "Mr Briggs,"
concluded the Solicitor-General, "is robbed and murdered in
a railway carriage; the murderer takes from him his watch and
chain, and takes from him his hat. All the articles taken are
found on Müller; he gives a false statement of how he got
them, and the hat left behind is the hat of Müller." If these
circumstances were proved by witnesses, then, in the opinion
of the Solicitor-General, a stronger case of circumstantial
evidence had rarely, if ever, been submitted to a jury.

The first witnesses called were those concerned in the
finding of Mr Briggs and the medical gentlemen who had
examined his body. It was with the appearance of Death, the
jeweller, that the real interest of the case began. Death was
clear that it was Müller who had brought him Mr Briggs's
chain on 11 July, which he had valued at £3 10s. Müller said
that he would prefer to take another chain in exchange instead
of money, upon which Death gave him a gold chain worth £3
5s, and a 5s. ring to make up the balance. The chain he had

put into a box identical with that which the prisoner had given to Matthews's little girl. In cross-examination it was suggested to Death that Müller had been to his shop in the previous year, but Death and his brother were positive that they had neither of them seen the prisoner before 11 July.

Mrs Blyth, Müller's landlady, gave evidence as to the prisoner's movements at the time of the murder. In cross-examination she bore testimony to the quiet and inoffensive disposition of the prisoner. She said that owing to an injury to his foot, Müller was wearing a slipper on one foot the day of the murder, and she admitted that he had spoken of going to America some fortnight before the murder of Mr Briggs. Her evidence was supported by that of her husband.

Mrs Repsch, the wife of a German tailor, a fellow-workman with Müller, gave important evidence. Müller had been at their house the evening of the murder, and had left them about half-past seven or eight o'clock. On Monday, the 11th, Müller had shown Mrs Repsch the chain which Death had given him in exchange for that of Mr Briggs. He had told her what was not true: that he had bought it in the docks. She noticed that he was wearing a different hat. Müller said he had bought it for 14s 6d., upon which her husband had remarked that it looked more like a guinea hat. She recollected the hat which Müller had been wearing previous to this. To the best of her belief it was the hat found in the railway carriage. Cross-examined, Mrs Repsch said that she particularly remembered this hat because of its peculiar lining.

John Haffa, a journeyman tailor, and friend of the prisoner, deposed to having pawned his own coat on the Wednesday before Müller sailed for America in order to help his friend to buy his passage; but in cross-examination he admitted that before 9 July he had seen Müller in possession of a sum of money sufficient to have paid for his passage.

On the second day of the trial the Crown commenced by calling evidence as to the exact financial position of Müller immediately before and after the murder. It then appeared that in June Müller had raised £3 by pawning a gold watch and chain at the shop of a Mrs Barker, in Houndsditch. On

Monday, 11 July, he got from Death in exchange for Mr Briggs's chain a gold chain valued at £3 5s. This he pawned on the Tuesday for £1 10s., and with the money so obtained he took his own watch out of pawn from Mrs Barker's. By borrowing £1 from a man of the name of Glass he redeemed his own chain also, which he had left with Mrs Barker. Glass and he then pawned this watch and chain a second time with Messrs Cox, of Princes Street, Leicester Square, for a sum of £4. This pawn ticket Müller sold to Glass for 5s.; thus Müller had altogether £4 5s., and it was with this sum that he had purchased his passage to America. If Müller were the murderer of Mr Briggs, he had perjured his soul for the paltry sum of thirty shillings.

The evidence of Jonathan Matthews, cabman, was awaited with some excitement. His severe cross-examination at the Police Court by Mr Beard had led to the expectation that the defence might seek to prove Müller's innocence of the murder by suggesting Matthews as having been the guilty man. But Serjeant Parry was wise enough not to adopt so dangerous a course. His cross-examination was directed entirely to damage the credit of Matthews as a trustworthy witness. Matthews identified the hat found in the carriage as one with a peculiar striped lining, which he had bought for Müller at his own request at Mr Walker's, in Crawford Street. Serjeant Parry showed that on the question of his purchases of hats Matthews's statements at the trial differed materially from those he had made before the coroner and the magistrate, and he questioned him pointedly as to what had become of his own old hats, particularly the one which he had bought at Mr Walker's, the one to which Müller had taken such a fancy that he had asked him to get him another like it. At the Police Court Matthews could give no account of his movements on the night of Mr Brigg's murder. Now he said he had made inquiries, and had found that he had been on the cab-stand at Paddington station from seven to eleven o'clock. Matthews adhered to the statement that he knew nothing of the murder until 18 July, when he saw near his cab-stand the bill offering a reward for the apprehension of the murderer. He denied that it was a desire to receive the £300 reward that had prompted him to give his evidence against Müller.

A new fact Serjeant Parry elicited as damaging to Matthews's good character, though it cannot be said that it told very heavily against his credibility as a witness in this particular instance. In 1850, at the age of nineteen, Matthews had undergone twenty-one days' imprisonment for theft. He had been at that time conductor of a coach at Norwich, and had absconded from his situation, taking with him in his box a bit, a spur, and a padlock belonging to his employer. Matthews preferred to describe this incident as a "spree", which, he said, had been construed harshly into an act of theft, and he protested that the things had been put into his box "unbeknown" to him. He had never been in trouble since. Severe as was the cross-examination of Matthews, in the judgment of those who heard it, it had not shaken the weight of his evidence in any material degree.

Mrs Matthews gave evidence as to the jewellers' box given by Müller to her little daughter. In cross-examination she admitted that she had known of Mr Briggs's murder on the Monday following, though her husband would appear to have known nothing of it until 18 July.

One fact came out unexpectedly in the evidence of Walker, the hatter, and his foreman. They stated that the lining in Müller's hat, which Matthews had bought for him at their shop, was very peculiar in character, and had not been used by them in the lining of more than two, or, at most, three or four hats.

The evidence of the police officers who had arrested Müller in New York was followed by that of Mr Briggs's son and his hatter, Digance. Mr Thomas Briggs identified both the watch and hat found in Müller's box as having belonged to his father. Digance said that as Mr Briggs had found his last hat a little too easy on the head, he had placed a piece of tissue paper inside the lining; some small fragments of this tissue paper were remaining in the band of the hat when found in Müller's box.

It was half-past two when Serjeant Parry rose to make his

speech for the defence. He spoke for two hours and a half. It was the only speech then allowed by law, and the Serjeant complained with some reason that, though he was about to call evidence for the defence, he was forbidden to sum up his case to the jury, a privilege that would have been accorded him if he had been engaged at *nisi prius* "in some miserable squabble between a hackney cab and a dust cart". By "Denman's Act", passed in the following year, the grievance alluded to by the learned serjeant was removed.

The serjeant commenced by dealing with the evidence that had been called for the Crown. He warned the jury that, though they might be satisfied that Müller had had a hat similar to that found in the carriage, they must not therefore assume that the hat found in the carriage had necessarily belonged to Müller. He deprecated warmly any intention of accusing Matthews of the murder. At the same time, he suggested that the hat found in the carriage might just as well have been Matthews's as Müller's. Matthews he described as an entirely unreliable witness, actuated solely by the desire to obtain the £300 reward, and proved in one instance to have lied deliberately before both magistrate and coroner.

As regards Mr Briggs's hat, he commented on the fact that the prosecution had called no witness to prove that, on the day of his death, Mr Briggs was wearing such a hat as that found on Müller. Müller's false statement as to the way he had become possessed of the watch and chain he attributed to the fact that the prisoner had bought them at the docks under circumstances which must have convinced him that he was buying them from some person who had obtained possession of them in a suspicious way. He pointed out, and very justly, that no bloodstained clothes had been found on Müller, and that the evidence given to prove that he had changed or got rid of some of his clothes after the murder was highly inconclusive. He scouted the idea that a slight and by no means muscular young man such as the prisoner could in three minutes, the time taken by the train to go from Bow to Hackney Wick station, have murdered, robbed, and thrown out of the carriage a man 5 feet 9 inches in height and weighing 12 stone. The crime, he contended, and he was going to call evidence to prove it, must have been the work of two men. Nor would he accept the Solicitor-General's suggestion that Mr Briggs's stick had been the weapon with which the crime had been committed. "A pair of shears," he said, "had been taken out of the pocket of the prisoner; he did not suppose that even now the Solicitor-General would suggest that the murder was committed with them." A curious comment on this statement is contained in a letter written to *The Times* two days after Müller's execution by Mr Toulmin, the surgeon who had made the post-mortem on Mr Briggs. In this letter Mr Toulmin expressed the opinion that the "tailor's shears found on Müller, some 13 inches or 14 inches long, and weighing about 2 lbs., was the only instrument he knew of that might have inflicted the wounds found on Mr Briggs", and he quoted the statement of a journeyman tailor to the effect that a tailor who did not take away his shears every day from his workshop would very quickly lose them.

Serjeant Parry said that he should call as the first witness for the defence a Mr Lee, a respectable gentleman who had given evidence at the inquest, but for some reason had not been called by the Crown. Mr Lee would say that he had seen Mr Briggs in a compartment of a first-class carriage at Fenchurch Street station on the night of 9 July; that, knowing him, he had said "Good-night" to him, and that he had then seen two men sitting in the carriage with him. The serjeant said that he should further prove an alibi; he would prove that between nine and ten o'clock on the night of Mr Briggs's murder Müller had been at a house in James Street, Camberwell. He would also call an omnibus conductor, who would swear that about ten minutes to ten on the Saturday night a passenger had got on to his omnibus at Camberwell Gate, wearing a carpet slipper on one foot. He was not prepared to swear that the passenger was Müller, but it had been proved by the prosecution that, owing to the injury to his foot, Müller was wearing a slipper on that night, and, if he were at Camberwell Gate at ten minutes to ten, it was clear that he could not have left Fenchurch by the 9.50 train.

At the conclusion of the learned serjeant's speech the Court adjourned until nine o'clock on Saturday, 29 October, when Mr Thomas Lee, the first witness for the defence, was called. Mr Lee swore that he had seen Mr Briggs sitting with two other men in a first-class compartment of the 9.50 train from Fenchurch Street on the night of the murder. He swore that he had said, "Good-night, Mr Briggs," to which Mr Briggs had replied, "Good-night, Tom." He could not swear to the prisoner being either of the men. Mr Lee was positive and unshaken on the main point of his evidence, in spite of a severe cross-examination. When asked why he had not made his statement to the police until more than a week after the murder, he answered that it was because he thought it unimportant, and knew what a bother it would be. "I have something to do," he said; "I collect my own rents" — a frame of mind which the Chief Baron, with some reason, declared threw general discredit upon Mr Lee's views and motives.

After some evidence that the cutting down and stitching of hats was a usual method of procedure in the second-hand hat trade, the defence proceeded with the proof of the prisoner's alibi. This rested on the evidence of a girl of the unfortunate class, and that of the man and woman in whose house she lived. Müller had formed an intimacy with the girl Eldred, and, according to the evidence of Mr and Mrs Jones, with whom the poor girl lodged, Müller had called at their house in Camberwell at half past nine o'clock on the night of 9 July. The girl Eldred was out, and Müller had remained talking to Mrs Jones for five to ten minutes, after which he had left. If the evidence of Mrs Jones was absolutely correct, then Müller could not have reached Fenchurch Street from Camberwell in time to have caught the 9.50 train. But the prosecution suggested that her evidence was not strictly correct. It had been proved that Müller had left his friend Haffa at Jewry Street at eight o'clock that night. If he had gone straight from there to Camberwell he would have reached there about nine, the hour at which he must have known the girl Eldred was in the habit of going out. If that were so, he would then have had plenty of time to get on an omnibus to Fenchurch Street, possibly arriving at that station at the same time as Mr Briggs. The character of Mr and Mrs Jones did not help their credibility, and the Solicitor-General dwelt with almost undue vehemence on the little reliance that was to be placed on the clock of a brothel; it is difficult to see why the veracity of a clock should vary according to the character of the house in which it stands. The girl Eldred, whom the Chief Baron described as a pathetic figure, heard and seen with great compassion, had evidently done her best to save the life of the young man, and, as she left the court, Müller looked at her with an expression of sincere gratitude.

The evidence of the omnibus conductor as to his passenger wearing slippers was quite valueless.

The Solicitor-General exercised his right to reply. He dealt very severely with the evidence that had been called for the defence, and reiterated the great strength of the case that had been made out by the Crown. At half-past one the Chief Baron commenced his charge to the jury. It occupied a little more than an hour and a quarter. Though scrupulously fair and dignified in tone, it was decidedly unfavourable to the prisoner. It was clear that the learned judge was powerfully impressed by the strength of the circumstantial evidence against the prisoner. Müller listened to the charge with painful anxiety. The jury, who declined the offer of the Chief Baron to read through to them the whole of the evidence, were only absent from the court a quarter of an hour, when they returned with a verdict of guilty. Baron Martin, as the junior judge, passed sentence of death. "I have no more doubt," he said to Müller, "that you committed this murder than I have with reference to the occurrence of any other event of which I am certain, but which I did not see with my own eyes." At the conclusion of the sentence the prisoner was understood to say, "I should like to say something; I am satisfied with the sentence which your lordship has passed. I know very well that it is what the law of the country prescribes. What I have to say is that I have not been convicted on a true statement of the facts, but on a false statement." As he left the dock his firmness gave way, and he burst into tears.

No sooner had Müller been condemned to die than the German Society made strenuous efforts to obtain a remission of the sentence. A memorial was prepared for presentation to the Home Secretary, Sir George Grey. Even the King of Prussia and some of the minor German potentates had telegraphed to the Queen asking her to intervene and save Müller's life.

The execution had been fixed for Tuesday, 14 November. On 10 November the German Society presented their memorial to Sir George Grey. They relied, among other things, on a story of a parcel which had been thrown from a cab into the bedroom of a Mr Poole at Edmonton, breaking his window at two o'clock in the morning of Sunday, 10 July. Mr Poole had followed the cab with a view to obtaining compensation for the damage done to his window. There were four men inside the cab, one without a hat, and wearing a handkerchief round his head. The parcel that had been thrown contained bloodstained trousers. But the matter resolved itself into nothing more than a foolish spree. The memorial also included a statement of a Baron de Camin, who said that he had seen a bloodstained man on the Embankment between Bow and Hackney Wick station on the night of 9 July. Müller had, since his confinement, made a statement to the effect that he had bought the hat found on him at Mr Digance's shop, but Digance and his shopman, when confronted with Müller in Newgate, failed to recognize him. On 8 November Mr and Mrs Blyth, with whom Müller had lodged, and who had evidently become rather attached to the young man, made a declaration at Worship Street Police Court that Müller had been wearing the same hat on the Sunday as he had been wearing on the Saturday, the day of the crime. They said that they had not seen the hat produced at the trial, but were sure that it was not his hat. These efforts to save Müller were not allowed to go without reply. An attempt was made, but fruitlessly, to connect Müller with the murder, in 1863, of Emma Jackson, a woman of light character, killed in a house of ill-fame in George Street, Bloomsbury. The unfortunate girl had been found dead about four o'clock on the afternoon of 10 April. No clue was ever obtained to the murderer, though there were people living in an adjoining room, and almost immediately below, at the time the crime must have been committed. One or two Germans wrote to the newspapers protesting against any reflections that had been made on English justice in connection with Müller's trial, and saying that they were perfectly satisfied that he had been fairly tried, and had no wish to interfere with his punishment.

Mr Beard received Sir George Grey's reply to the memorial on Saturday, 11 November. In it Sir George Grey stated that, after carefully comparing the statements contained in the memorial with the evidence given at the trial, and, after communicating fully with the two judges who had tried the case, he could see no ground for advising Her Majesty to remit the death penalty. At three o'clock in the afternoon Mr Beard called at Newgate and acquainted Müller with the Home Secretary's decision. Müller received the news with calmness and composure, and expressed his gratitude for the efforts that had been made to save his life. In spite of the efforts of Dr Cappel, the German Lutheran minister attending upon him, Müller refused to make any statement by way of confession, and appeared to be perfectly prepared to meet his fate. His public execution on 14 November furnished a scene more disgraceful than usual. The crowd, consisting of a mob of the lowest kind, kept up their spirits during the night by shouting and singing doggerel verses alluding to the murderer. On the evening of the 13th Müller was visited by one of the sheriffs, who again exhorted him to confess, but Müller obstinately declared his innocence. As the sheriff left he turned to one of the warders and said, "Man has no power to forgive sins, and there is no use in confessing them to him." He was equally obdurate on the morning of his execution while Dr Cappel was praying with him. He mounted the scaffold calmly, looked with curiosity at the beam above his head, and, though trembling a little, showed no sign of fear. Immediately before the drop fell, Dr Cappel once again besought Müller to admit his guilt, when the following conversation took place between them:

Dr Cappel — Müller, in a few moments you will stand before God. I ask you again, and for the last time, are you guilty or not guilty?

Müller — Not guilty.

Dr Cappel — You are not guilty?

Müller — God knows what I have done.

Dr Cappel — God knows what you have done. Does he also know that you have committed this crime?

Müller — Yes, I have done it. (*Ja, ich habe es gethan.*)

It is difficult at this distance of time to quite appreciate the extraordinary interest that the case of Müller aroused. There is nothing very remarkable either in the crime or in the criminal. The trial itself is interesting as showing the conclusive weight of circumstantial evidence. That it did create extraordinary interest at the time there can be no doubt. It was the first railway murder, and the circumstances of the flight and capture of the murderer were calculated to excite the public mind. The character of Müller is a little difficult to understand. He would seem to have been a young man who could make friends among both men and women; all the witnesses at his trial spoke of his humane and gentle disposition. He was, however, at times overbearing and inclined to violence. He was vain, and in the habit of making boastful and untrue statements about himself and his doings. He seems to have been fond of jewellery, and it is probably correct to surmise, as Baron Martin said in sentencing him to death, that, "moved by the devil in the shape of Mr Briggs's gold watch and albert chain, the young man was overcome with a sudden impulse of greed", to which he yielded the more readily owing to his desire to obtain sufficient money to take him to America, where he seems to have thought that he would be more successful than in England.

*Murder*
*by a*
*Dandy*

Montagu Williams, QC

I SUPPOSE that the most sensational trial that I ever was engaged in during my career at the Bar was that of Percy Mapleton, *alias* Lefroy — described in the calendar as a journalist — who was tried in the Maidstone Assizes before the Lord Chief Justice (Sir John Coleridge) on 5 November 1881. The Attorney-General (Sir Henry James, Q.C., M.P.), Mr Harry Poland, and Mr A.L. Smith conducted the prosecution. I, with Mr Forrest Fulton and Mr Kisch, was specially retained by Mr Duerdin Dutton to defend the accused.

The murder took place on 27 June, and it had attracted a great deal of public attention. In fact, in the interval that had elapsed, it had been a universal topic of conversation.

Before the magistrates at Cuckfield, Sussex, the prisoner had been prosecuted by the Treasury authorities, and defended by his solicitor, Mr Dutton. He had been committed to take his trial at the Autumn Assizes at Maidstone, Kent.

The prisoner was an extraordinary-looking young man of about twenty-two years of age. He wore a black frock-coat, tightly buttoned up, a low stand-up collar, and a dark cravat. He carried a brand-new silk hat in his hand. Upon entering the dock from the cells below, he made a low bow to the Chief Justice. He was at once called upon to plead to the indictment, "for that he was accused of the wilful murder of Frederick Isaac Gold upon 27 June". He replied, in a voice so inaudible that it was a whisper, "I am not guilty." He was told that the time had come for him to make any objection to the jury, if objection he had to make; whereupon he bowed towards the jury-box, evidently with a desire to intimate that he was perfectly satisfied with its occupants. While the jury were being sworn, Lefroy stood listlessly with his hands behind him. Though self-possessed, it was clear that he was nervous.

Before the Attorney-General commenced his speech, the

prisoner placed his hat on a ledge at the side of the dock. He took it up again, and then once more returned it to the ledge. Apparently, he was loth to part with it. It subsequently transpired that Lefroy was a man of considerable conceit. On the first morning of his trial, he actually asked for his dress-coat, in order that he might wear that garment in the dock. He was, in a word, a man steeped in a kind of petty, strutting, theatrical vanity. Nevertheless, it was almost inexplicable that he should devote more attention to his hat than to the proceedings of the trial.

The peculiarity was not confined to the opening day. Every morning, on taking his place in the dock, he put his hat down with the greatest circumspection, in the exact spot that he had originally selected for it; and every afternoon, when the Court adjourned, he took it up again with infinite care.

As will be seen from the evidence, the hat he wore at the time of the murder was missing, and the one he now cherished so fondly in the dock was a brand-new one, and had evidently been given to him by a friend during his incarceration.

It was curious to note the change that took place in Lefroy's bearing and demeanour whenever he caught sight of an artist from one of the illustrated papers in the act of sketching him. He suddenly brightened up, and, if I am not mistaken, assumed a studied pose for the occasion.

The Attorney-General, in opening the case to the jury, occupied about three hours. After stating the nature of the charge against the prisoner, he proceeded to give an outline of the evidence he was about to produce.

It appeared that the murdered man, Mr Gold, had lived in the suburbs of Brighton and was sixty-four years of age. He had been engaged in business in London, but had retired some time before, retaining a pecuniary interest in one shop. Every Monday morning he proceeded to the metropolis for the purpose of receiving from his manager, Mr Cross, his share of the weekly profits of that shop. Sometimes he took the money straight to his London bankers, and sometimes he carried it to his seaside home. On Monday, 27 June, Mr Gold left his home at five minutes past eight to proceed by train to London, where he would arrive shortly before ten. He was dressed in his usual way, and carried in his pocket a watch with a white face, made by a person named Griffiths and bearing the number 16, 261. On arriving in London, he proceeded to the shop, and received from Mr Cross a sum of £38 5s. 6d. He then went to his bank, which was the eastern branch of the London and Westminster, and there deposited the sum of £38.

Mr Gold was next heard of at the London Bridge station of the London, Brighton and South Coast Railway, where he arrived shortly before two o'clock. He was a season-ticket holder on the line, and was well known to the officials at the station. He entered the express train which left London Bridge at two o'clock, taking his seat in a carriage that contained four compartments. One was a second-class, another a first-class smoking, another a first-class, and the last a second-class. It was in the first-class smoking compartment that Mr Gold was seen by the ticket-collector to take his seat. Just before the train started, another passenger was seen to join him. By that train only three first-class tickets were issued from London to Brighton. Two of them were issued to a lady, and were subsequently accounted for. The third, which was numbered 3, 181, had been traced to the prisoner.

The train reached Croydon Station at twenty-three minutes past two. Eight miles from Croydon was a tunnel of about a mile in length, and as the train approached the entrance of that tunnel, the attention of a passenger named Gibson, a chemist, was attracted by the sound of four explosions. He imagined they were fog signals. After the train had run a further distance of eight miles, it reached a place called Horley. Close to the line there were some cottages, and outside one of them stood a Mrs Brown and her daughter. As the train passed, they saw, in one of the compartments, two persons standing up and struggling together. Whether or not the two persons were merely larking, Mrs Brown and her daughter could not say. Seven miles further on was Balcombe Tunnel, and, after passing through that tunnel, the train stopped at a place called Preston Park, which is about a mile from Brighton Station.

After the train had drawn up at the platform, the attention of the ticket-collector was called to the prisoner, who still occupied the same carriage that both he and Mr Gold had entered at the commencement of the journey. The prisoner was found in a dishevelled condition, and smothered with gore. Apparently he was wounded in the head. His collar was gone. A quantity of blood was bespattered about the compartment. Lefroy asked for a policeman, and made a statement to the ticket-collector. He declared that, when he commenced the journey from London, two persons had been in the carriage with him. One of them he described as an elderly man, and the other as a countryman of about fifty years of age. He went on to say that, as the train entered the tunnel, he was attacked by, he believed, the elderly man, that he became insensible, and that he knew nothing of what occurred until just before the train arrived at Preston Park.

When he alighted upon the platform, attention was called to the fact that a watch-chain was hanging from his shoe. The prisoner explained that he had placed it there for safety. Upon the chain being removed, it was found that a watch was attached to it. He was allowed to retain possession of those articles.

The prisoner was taken to the Town Hall at Brighton, where he made a statement. From the Town Hall he was removed to the hospital, and after remaining there for some time, in the custody of two policemen, he was permitted to return to his place of residence at Wallington, near Croydon. The house at Wallington was the home of his second cousin.

At a quarter to four on the Monday, some forty-five minutes after the train had passed through Balcombe Tunnel, a platelayer came upon the body of Mr Gold, lying near the entrance. The marks on the corpse left no doubt that the unfortunate gentleman had been shot. Subsequently, indeed, a bullet was found in his neck. The body was further disfigured with wounds that had apparently been inflicted by a knife; and from the nature of those injuries the conclusion might be drawn that a long and deadly struggle had taken place between Mr Gold and his assailant.

At a quarter past five, another platelayer, working on the line some distance nearer Brighton, found a shirt-collar. As already stated, when the prisoner arrived at Brighton, he was without one. He had, indeed, in company with a policeman, gone to a shop in Brighton, and purchased a new one; and it was afterwards seen that the collar found and the collar purchased were of the same size.

At five minutes past three, at a place called Burgess Hill, which was situated some forty-two miles from London, a hat was discovered on the up-line, and, at a place called Hassock's Gate, a young woman working in a field some yards from the railway found an umbrella which, as was afterwards proved, had belonged to Mr Gold. The watch taken from the prisoner's shoe was also found to have been the property of the murdered man.

Three Hanoverian medals, which somewhat resembled sovereigns, were found in the carriage from which the prisoner alighted at Preston Park, and, according to the testimony of persons with whom Lefroy had resided, he had been in the habit of carrying such medals about with him. Nevertheless, when questioned on the point, he denied all knowledge of the three that had been found.

It was known that, on the day of the murder, Lefroy had a revolver in his possession. Some time previously it had been pawned for five shillings by a person giving the name of William Lee. On 27 June — the day on which Mr Gold was murdered — the pledge had been redeemed. The prisoner was alleged to be the man who pawned the revolver and afterwards reclaimed it. After taking out the weapon, sufficient time would have been left him to proceed to London Bridge station and catch the train.

Besides the hat belonging to Mr Gold that was found upon the line, a second hat was discovered there, and this was of the same shape, make, and size as the one Lefroy was in the habit of wearing.

The accused was accompanied, on his return journey from Brighton, by two policemen. At one of the places where the train stopped, an official of the company entered the carriage, and, speaking so as to be heard by the accused, stated that a body had been found in the tunnel. This information seemed to determine the accused as to his future movements.

After the two constables had quitted the house at Wallington, whither they conducted Lefroy, he told the servant that he was going out in order to visit a surgeon in the neighbourhood. As a matter of fact, he never went to any doctor at all. What became of him during the next few days was shrouded in mystery. It was known, however, that on Thursday, the 30th, he made his appearance at the house of a Mrs Bickers, in Smith Street, Stepney, where lodgings were to let. At that time there was, of course, a hue-and-cry after him. He gave a false name, and stated that he had come from Liverpool, and that he was an engineer. He remained at the house for a week. He only went out of doors once or twice, and it was clear to its other inmates that he had no occupation.

While lodging in Smith Street, he caused somebody to take a telegram for him to the Post Office. The mysterious message was sent in the name of Clarke to a Mr Seal, at an office in Gresham Street. It ran as follows: "Please send my wages tonight without fail about eight o'clock. Flour to-morrow. Not 33."

On the evening of the day on which the telegram was sent, two police officers, one of whom was Inspector Swanson, called at the house in Smith Street, and took Lefroy into custody. In his room a false beard was discovered.

The first day of the trial was occupied by the Attorney-General's address, and by the brief examination of one or two witnesses.

So far, the proceedings apparently made little impression upon Lefroy, for beyond every now and then lifting his eyelids, he made no sign. At times, indeed, he seemed to be dozing.

The jury, which was composed of twelve quiet-looking men, evidently drawn from agricultural scenes, clearly took the profoundest interest in the proceedings. Some of them from time to time jotted down notes.

# MURDER.
# £200 REWARD.

WHEREAS, on Monday, June 27th, ISAAC FREDERICK GOULD was murdered on the London Brighton and South Coast Railway, between Three Bridges and Balcombe, in East Sussex

AND WHEREAS a Verdict of WILFUL MURDER has been returned by a Coroner's Jury against

## PERCY LEFROY MAPLETON,
whose Portrait and Handwriting are given hereon,—

and who is described as being 22 years of age, height 5 ft 8 or 9 in., very thin, hair (cut short) dark, small dark whiskers; dress, dark frock coat, and shoes, and supposed low black hat (worn at back of head), had scratches from fingers on throat, several wounds on hea t, the dressing of which involved the cutting of hair, recently lodged at 4, Cathcart Road, Wallington, was seen at 9.30 a.m. 28th ult., with his head bandaged, at the Fever Hospital, Liverpool Road, Islington. Had a gold open-faced watch (which he is likely to pledge). "Maker, Griffiths, Mile End Road, No 16261."

One Half of the above Reward will be paid by Her Majesty's Government, and One Half by the Directors of the London Brighton and South Coast Railway to any person (other than a person belonging to a Police Force in the United Kingdom) who shall give such information as shall lead to the discovery and apprehension of the said PERCY LEFROY MAPLETON, or others, the Murderer, or Murderers, upon his or their conviction; and the Secretary of State for the Home Department will advise the grant of Her Majesty's gracious PARDON to any accomplice, not being the person who actually committed the Murder, who shall give such evidence as shall lead to a like result.

Information to be given to the Chief Constable of East Sussex, Lewes, at any Police Station, or to

### The Director of Criminal Investigations, Gt. Scotland Yard.

JULY 4th, 1881.

(4313)        Harrison and Sons, Printers in Ordinary to Her Majesty, St. Martin's Lane.

*Reproduction of a Handbill in the Lefroy case.*

On the second day, the Police Superintendent of Lewes gave evidence as to the wish expressed by the prisoner to wear the dress-coat. The subject at once aroused the interest of Lefroy, and he listened intently to what passed.

"He asked me," said the superintendent, "to let him have the pawn-ticket for his dress-coat, as he wished to appear in it at the trial."

The persons in court smiled, and no wonder. The picture presented to the mind, of the prisoner, arrayed in evening dress, standing behind the spiked bars of the dock, was irresistibly ludicrous. Apparently, Lefroy plumed himself not a little on the possession of a dress-coat. Perhaps in his mind evening clothes denoted extraordinary respectability. Of all his worldly goods, they were certainly the last he parted with; and of all his wardrobe, they were in the best condition. When he did pawn them, it was only under pressure of absolute want. What effect he supposed his appearance in a dress-coat in the early morning would have had upon the minds of the jury, I do not profess to understand.

On the third day of the trial, which was a Monday, the case for the prosecution closed, and, at about eleven o'clock, I rose to address the jury for the defence. My speech lasted for about three hours, and I do not think that I ever saw a jury more attentive. Some of them gave way to tears.

Once, Lefroy shifted his chair a little, and seemed for the moment as though he really intended to wake up and listen. This was a mere spasmodic effort, however, and it soon died away. He either had no interest in the business in hand, or he took care to disguise it.

I endeavoured in the first instance to show the weakness of the prosecution in failing to connect Lefroy with the knowledge of Mr Gold's habits. I commented on the testimony of the various witnesses and endeavoured to show that, though the evidence was strongly circumstantial, the prosecution had failed to establish the fact, beyond any doubt, that the murder was actually committed by the prisoner.

A curious circumstance occurred while I was dealing with the evidence of a man named Weston, a member of the

Brighton Town Council. Upon my describing him as a fabricator of evidence, he jumped up in Court and, with his arms moving about like the sails of a windmill, demanded an instant hearing. The only satisfaction he obtained was the curt answer from the Bench: "I shall have to order you to be removed if you do not be silent."

The Attorney-General — who is the only man at the Bar, save his representative, the Solicitor-General, who has a prescriptive right to reply to a defence where no witnesses are called — in a speech of two hours' duration, calmly, and without any display of rhetoric, save at rare intervals, proceeded to comment upon the whole of the proceedings. He produced rather a dramatic effect when, with his fingers pointed towards the prisoner at the bar, he alluded to him as "a fellow-creature standing on the very brink of the precipice of his fate". I am bound to say, however, that, as a whole, his speech was unimpassioned and judicial. It was very earnest, was marked by cogency and closeness of reasoning, and was full of hard, destructive facts. He begged the jury to dismiss all sentiment, and appealed strongly to their reason. No fact that could be brought into view was missed, and no symptom was given of a desire to distort the evidence. At half-past five he concluded his address, and the Judge adjourned, to sum up the case on the morrow.

It subsequently transpired that, when Lefroy quitted the dock that evening, he was so confident as to the result of the trial being in his favour, that he turned to the gaoler, and said: "When I am acquitted, I hope I shan't be mobbed."

Both the Attorney-General and myself had to proceed to London that night. We went up to town in the same railway-compartment, and chatted over the case on the journey. He said to me:

"You have won your verdict; that fellow will be acquitted."

I shook my head. I had noticed that, whatever effect my speech might have made upon the jury, the Chief Justice, during its delivery, occupied himself by making copious notes for his summing-up; and I knew that he intended to answer me on every point.

"Wait till to-morrow," I said, "you've not heard the Judge yet. Lefroy is a doomed man."

On the following morning, my anticipation as to the nature of the summing-up was fulfilled. It was a most deadly one. His lordship spoke from the sitting of the court until five-and-twenty minutes to three.

The jury, after a short retirement, returned a verdict of "Guilty", and the prisoner was sentenced to death.

During the absence of the jury, I noticed that the prisoner, whose life was hanging in the balance, showed symptoms of nervousness for the first time. His hands seemed to come mechanically to his face, his fingers twitched as he tugged at his moustache, and he moved uneasily in his chair, being evidently unable to control his emotion. Once or twice he got up from his seat, leant over the bars of the dock, and addressed a few words to his solicitor, Mr Dutton; then, as if by a great effort of will, he sat down again, and was comparatively calm.

When the foreman pronounced the word "Guilty", up rose Lefroy, and, placing his hands behind him, advanced to the rails. He seemed to be altogether at his ease, though pallid. There was a moment, however, when he grasped convulsively at the rails, and swayed to and fro, as though about to fall. But the weakness was only for a moment. The next minute he was himself again, and, folding his arms, he fixed his eyes intently upon the jury.

Just before he left the dock, he stretched out his right arm, in a theatrical way, towards the jury, and said:

"Some day you will learn, when too late, that you have murdered me." Then, with a firm step, he retired, and disappeared from the public gaze.

Two extraordinary letters — one of them written by Lefroy, evidently while he was in prison; the other being the answer thereto — came into my hands.

Lefroy's letter runs as follows:

My Darling Annie,

I am getting this posted secretly by a true and kind friend, and I trust you implicitly to do as I ask you. Dearest, should God permit a verdict of "Guilty" to be returned, you know what my fate must be unless you prevent it, which you can do by assisting me in this way. Send me (concealed in a common meat pie, made in an oblong tin cheap dish) saw file, six inches or so long, without a handle; place this at bottom of pie, embedded in under crust and gravy. And now, dearest, for the greater favour of the two. Send me, in centre of a small cake, like your *half-crown* one, a tiny bottle of prussic acid, the smaller the better; this last you could, I believe, obtain from either Drs Green or Cressy for *destroying a favourite cat*. My darling, believe me when I say, as *I hope for salvation*, that this last should only be used the last night allowed me by the law *to live*, if it comes to that last extremity. Never, while a *chance of life remained*, would I use it, but only as a *last resource*. It would be no suicide in God's sight, I am sure. Dearest, I trust this matter to you to aid me. I will face my trial as an innocent man should, and I believe God will restore me to you once more after this fearful lesson; but should He not, the file would give me a chance of escaping with life, while if both failed, I should still save myself from dying a felon's death *undeserved*. By packing these, as I say, carefully, sending with them a tin of milk, etc., no risk will be incurred, as my things are, comparatively speaking, never examined. Get them yourself soon, and — [an indistinct word] and direct them in a feigned hand, without any accompanying note. If you receive this safely, and will aid me, by return send a postcard, saying: *"Dear P., Captain Lefroy has returned."* Send them by Friday morning at latest.

If not P.A., get arsenic powder from Hart or other (or through Mrs B.); wrap up in three or four pieces of paper.

God bless you, darling. I trust you trust me. I can conceal several small things about me in safety.

The other letter is as follows:

My Ever Dearest Percy,

I am writing this, hoping that Mr — will do me the great kindness of taking it to you, because I may not have another opportunity. First I must tell you that the delay about what you mentioned has happened through our being told that only two shops in London make them, but trust before you have this it will have arrived safely; if so, say in your next: "The little basket with butter, etc., came safely." As to the other thing, oh, my darling, my heart is almost torn with the agony as to what to do about it. To think that *I* should be the means of putting you out of the world, or to think that it is *I* who leave you to an awful fate. Darling, *can* a suicide *repent*? What is ANYTHING compared with our future happiness or misery? God *can* and WILL pardon A. ъ sins, the *blackest* and worst, if we are *only* sorry and believe in His power to save; but how about one that you have *no time* to be sorry in? In any case I could not get it from those you mention, nor the A.P. from Hart. If I were alone, *no risk* I incurred for YOUR SAKE I should *think of for a moment*; but it would be dreadful for the poor little ones were I taken from them for years, as I should surely be were it traced. I thought of Julia, but do not know whether it would be safe; say what you think. If the worst happens, shall we be allowed to see you once in a room? It would be time then. Darling, YOU KNOW I would do ANYTHING for you I *could*, or that would not be BAD FOR YOU; but your soul is dearer and more precious than your body, and my one great, indeed, *only* comfort will be in *looking forward* to the time when WE SHALL MEET AGAIN; my love, if it were not *for that hope, my misery* would be UNBEARABLE. Oh, DO TURN to Him in this time of awful trouble; His arms are open to you. Whatever the verdict of the world may be, our dear mothers *will rejoice* to have you; ONLY *confess* all you have to confess to *Him*, who is *able* to save to *the uttermost*, and *believe* in His love. You know you have done many wrong things, and might have gone from bad to worse if this frightful calamity had not stopped you. I *think certainly* you have had some bad friend, and would be glad to *know* this — was it *"Lambton"*? Are you shielding anybody? My theory is this — wanting means, the sight of the ... was a great temptation, and unexpected resistance caused the rest; if this is correct, some time or other say: "What you surmised in your last is, I fancy, correct," or something like that, so that I may understand. My own dear one, I cannot fancy it prearranged; but of course I know something about the ... that no one else does, and it is that in a great measure that fills me with such sickening dread and wretchedness for your sake. My darling, what did you want money *so much* for? Wouldn't it be a comfort to tell *some one* EVERYTHING you *know*? I would guard your honour as my own, and all would be *safe* with *me*. Think it over, and if what we dread happens, write me a few lines by Mr — , who, I *know*, will give it to me *un*opened. In *any case your name* and memory will ever be among those MOST LOVED and *cherished* by our dear little ones as well as ourselves, who know and love you now. Do you still wish for a likeness of V.C.? One thing more. Has anything I have ever said, or done, or left unsaid or undone, helped you to do wrong? I feel bitterly that I have not been the friend I might have been in speaking more openly, etc., but I feared to hurt your feelings. Good-bye, my dearest, dearest Percy. PRAY WITHOUT CEASING that you may yet be restored to us in this world. God bless and comfort you.

Your ever loving and heart-broken Annie

I have tried through Smith to get a *witness* [?] for third person, but as yet have failed. All I *can* do I will, you may be sure. My belief in your innocence is *genuine*, for I feel certain it was not intended. If by any merciful chance you succeeded with the implement, how should we know, to bring you *things*, etc.?

Lefroy's friends were in the habit of referring to him as a "shy, gentle, timid, good-natured boy". He appears to have been of a romantic disposition, and to have found his chief delight in the companionship of books. It is said that all his friends and relatives were very fond of him, and that they had been very anxious lest his delicate state of health, and the weakness of his constitution, should have unfitted him for hard study and physical labours. Lefroy was in the habit of constantly visiting the theatres, and he wrote one or two plays, which, however, did not prove successful. Nevertheless, he sometimes succeeded in getting little things accepted by small weekly papers.

According to a statement Lefroy left with the prison chaplain, he spent almost his last penny, on the day of the murder, on the railway ticket that placed him in a situation to commit the crime. He said he had no knowledge of Mr Gold's habits, and no particular reason for supposing that that gentleman had money or valuables in his possession.

Just before his execution, a document was handed, at his request, to one of his nearest relatives. In it he stated that he had been desperate, owing to his want of money, and that, upon the morning of the murder, he rose early with the intention of obtaining funds, even though his efforts to do so involved murder. From this document it appears that, on arriving at the railway station, he walked up and down the platform, and looked into all the carriages, in the hope of discovering a lady likely to have some money in her possession. He stated that he thought he might succeed in robbing a woman by threatening her, and added that if he could, in this way, have avoided murder, he would have done so. He felt, he said, that if he offered the lady the alternative of giving up her money or her life, she would at once have yielded up the former. He could have coerced her by pointing the pistol at her, and, if necessary, he could have dealt her a blow which would have caused her to swoon. Seeing no lady whose appearance betokened the possession of any considerable sum of money, he entered a carriage which contained one gentleman, and immediately nerved himself for the commission of murder. In conclusion, Lefroy admitted that the finding of the jury was just and right.

# *The Vauxhall Murder*

## Canon J.A.R. Brookes

ON THE early afternoon of Thursday, 17 January, in the year 1901, a certain Mrs Rhoda King took a third-class ticket at Southampton with the intention of alighting at Vauxhall, and from there making her way to the house of her sister, who was living in Battersea. She left her husband at work and her children at home, and set out alone on her journey by the 1.40 express. Her mind was probably occupied by small domestic matters, and with the condition in which she should find her sister; certainly no idea of the dreadful tragedy of which she was so shortly to be a spectator ever crossed her mind for a single second. Why should it? Western life is so well ordered, and all our needs and desires are so carefully catered for and met — nobody thinks of murder as a possibility in everyday life; it may be mentioned in the newspapers, it may happen to other people, but not to ourselves. Murder is, in fact, as Mrs Belloc Lowndes picturesquely put it, the one chink in the armour of civilization for which no provision is ever made.

Mrs King was alone till the train reached Eastleigh, but here she was joined by a fine young fellow, over six feet in height, and of a very powerful build. After another quarter of an hour Winchester was reached, and a third person entered the compartment — Mr William Pearson, a well-to-do farmer. All the characters for the fatal drama were now complete, and the express started on its long run to Vauxhall.

George Parker, who sat with a revolver in his pocket, watching the farmer, was only twenty-three years of age, but he had lived long enough in the world to do a good deal of mischief. He had been dismissed from the Army, committed a theft at the Lyceum Theatre for which the police were then searching for him, and just recently he had separated on Eastleigh platform from a married woman with whom he had been carrying on an intrigue for some days. He was desperately in need of money and had entered the train with a ticket which held good only up to Winchester, a fact which he well knew would be made manifest at Vauxhall, where in 1901 all tickets were still collected. Some days before, he had purchased the revolver, and he had been for some time meditating a crime.

As he sat eyeing the farmer, he concluded, from his prosperous appearance, that he would probably have plenty of money in his purse, and urged by need he determined to kill him and take whatever he might have. Of course, the presence of a third party was a great nuisance; he would be obliged to kill her, too, in order to avoid detection. These express trains had a lavatory in each carriage, and Parker withdrew for a few minutes, as the train reached Surbiton, to make preparations for the murder, probably in order to load the revolver. He had postponed the deed as long as he could, and he knew that it must be done at once or not at all. Mrs King was looking out of the window as he re-entered, and was more surprised than frightened when she heard the noise of a report, which she said seemed to her like a pop-gun; as she turned she heard another discharge and she felt something in her cheek. Seeing Parker with the revolver in his hand, she exclaimed: "My God! What have you done? Why ever did you do it?"

"I did it for money," was the reply. "I want some money. Have you got any?"

With the blood streaming down her face on to her hands and dress, she took out her purse, and in her excitement tendered him only a shilling, at the same time imploring him to save her life for the sake of her husband and children. Fearful of the blood dripping from her hands, he refused the shilling and began rifling the body of Mr Pearson, whom he had killed with his first shot. Having opened the farmer's purse, he offered Mrs King a sovereign, probably in order to implicate her in the crime, and purchase her silence.

"Is that any use to you?" he enquired. She declined the gift, but promised to remain silent about the murder if only he would spare her life.

"What shall I do," said he, "with this b—y thing?"

indicating the revolver. "How would it do to put it in the old bloke's hand so that people will think he killed himself?" But Mrs King, no doubt thinking of her own safety, urged him to throw it out of the window; the murderer flung it out just as the train was passing Nine Elms. As the train began to slow down as it neared Vauxhall, Parker opened the door and got his foot on the step. Directly the platform was reached he sprang out while the train was still in motion, rushed along the platform to the exit, thrust the ticket of which he had robbed Mr Pearson into the astonished ticket collector's hand, and sprang down the steps leading to the street and safety.

Meanwhile, poor Mrs King had sufficient strength and presence of mind to stagger on to the platform and call out: "Stop him; he's killed a man." It was too late to capture him on the platform, but several men were soon on his tracks, and as he took refuge by mistake in a coke retort he was soon obliged to surrender.

Mrs King, too, though terribly shaken by her awful experience, was well enough to give evidence at the trial. A defence of temporary insanity was set up, but he was found guilty of wilful murder and executed on 19 March. He confessed his crime; in fact, in face of the direct evidence he could not do otherwise, but he was so far from feeling any real contrition for his act that he expressed himself as sorry at not having killed Mrs King and thereby evaded capture. From his point of view, of course, her conduct seemed treacherous; but from the standpoint of the ordinary citizen she was to be congratulated on having done her duty.

In cases of that nature a person is absolved from keeping a promise extorted by menaces; we agree with Mr Grewgious in *Edwin Drood*, who held the view that: "If you could steal a march upon a brigand, or a wild beast, you had better do it".

*The Merstham*
*Tunnel*
*Mystery*

Hargrave Lee Adam

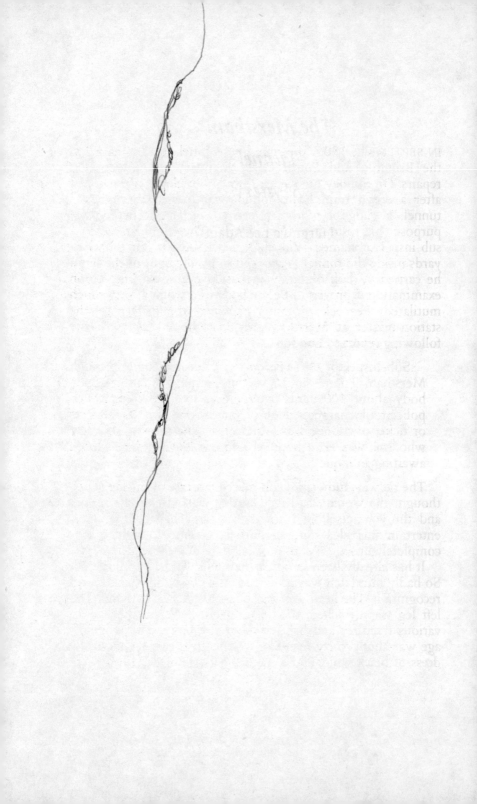

IN SEPTEMBER 1905, the mile-long tunnel at Merstham, on the Brighton and South Coast Railway, was undergoing repairs. On Sunday night, the 24th, about eleven o'clock, just after a down train from London had passed through the tunnel, a gang of workmen arrived on the scene for the purpose of resuming their work. The foreman was a sub-inspector named William Peacock. About four hundred yards inside the tunnel Peacock saw, by the light of the lamp he carried, a dark object lying beside the down line. Upon examination it proved to be the body of a woman, very much mutilated. Peacock promptly reported the matter to the station-master at Merstham station, who in turn sent the following report to London:

> Sub-Inspector W. Peacock, while walking through Merstham Tunnel, at 10.55 this evening, found a female body about 400 yards from the end of the tunnel. The police took charge of the body and searched it. No address or ticket or money was found on it, and nothing to show who she was. The body is lying at the Feathers Hotel, awaiting an inquest.

The railway authorities considered it a case of suicide. They thought the woman had deliberately walked into the tunnel and thrown herself in front of a train. They continued to entertain this idea until certain facts came to light which completely upset it. Let us proceed to review these facts.

It has already been said that the body was badly mutilated. So badly mutilated was it, indeed, as to be altogether beyond recognition. The head was smashed and the face battered. The left leg was detached, the left arm crushed, and there were various fractures and bruises about the body. The woman's age was about thirty-five. She was five feet two high, wore a dress of black voile, and a picture-hat trimmed with flowers

61

and a pink bow at the side. An arm pad, or dress-protector, was marked "Boston". There was no pocket in her dress. Her underclothing was marked with the figures "245" in pink on white cotton bands. She wore shabby patent-leather shoes, with revolving rubber heels. She was a strong, well-built woman, with dark-brown hair. She had small hands, which showed no signs of manual work. Her teeth were slightly discoloured and somewhat irregular. Two teeth were missing, one from each jaw and in corresponding positions. Round her neck was a gold chain, on which was a locket. There were several rings on her fingers. The only means of identification would be by means of the general appearance of the body, the clothing, or the laundry marks on the linen.

The most significant fact of all was the discovery of a gag in the mouth of the deceased. It was formed of a kind of scarf which she had herself apparently been wearing. It was so firmly fixed in the mouth that the police had some difficulty in removing it. There was an abrasion at the side of the mouth, also on the roof of the mouth, just beyond the teeth, apparently caused during the process of thrusting the gag into the mouth, either with a thumb or finger, or possibly the end of a stick. There was blood on the ground where the body was found. On the sooty wall of the tunnel, about five feet eight inches from the ground, were markings — long horizontal markings — showing where the deceased's head and hands had encountered it. This made it quite clear that the deceased had not, as the railway officials at first supposed, wandered into the tunnel, bent upon suicide, but had, in fact, been travelling in a train, which was passing through the tunnel, and been thrown or had fallen out of a carriage.

The position of the body made it clear that the train she was travelling in must have been a down train. The fact that the body was still warm proved that death had occurred recently — say within the last hour. It was the opinion of Dr Critchett, a local practitioner, who made an examination of the body and the tunnel where it lay, that the woman had been thrown out of the train, on the left-hand side, coming from London.,

He thought she must have come out of the carriage "full stretch", hands and feet sliding helplessly on the wall of the tunnel. After striking the wall, said Dr Critchett, she must have rebounded and fallen under the wheels of the train and so received her many injuries.

It was not long before the body of the unfortunate woman was identified. The following day a young man named Robert Henry Money, a dairy-farmer carrying on business at Kingston, viewed the body and identified it as that of his sister, a young woman of twenty-two, named Mary Sophia Money. She had been working as a book-keeper for Messrs Bridger & Co., dairymen, 245 Lavender Hill, Clapham Junction. The facts subsequently brought to light in connection with the identification did but serve to further deepen the mystery.

Miss Money, who was said to have been always of a bright and cheerful disposition, lived at her place of business. Every fourth Sunday she was on duty. On Sunday, 24 September, she was on duty. On that day she was in the company of another employee of Messrs Bridger's, a Miss Emma Hone, from 1 p.m. to 7p.m. At the latter hour Miss Money went out for, as she herself explained, "a little walk". She said she would not be long. She never came back.

She gave Miss Hone no information as to where she was going, or whether she intended to meet anybody, or call upon anybody. She was in her usual cheerful spirits. In her hand she carried her handkerchief, and in her handkerchief was her purse. Miss Hone was sure she had no pocket in her dress. She had no jacket on. Her purse was a small one, and seemed to be full of money, although Miss Hone could not say how much it contained. Miss Money was in the habit of returning on Sunday night by 10.30. The house closed at eleven. If she was later than that, somebody had to wait up for her.

On the night in question Miss Hone waited up for her till one in the morning. She then supposed that Miss Money had called on friends and missed the last train back. So she went to bed. It was unusual, by the way, for Miss Money to go out so late on a Sunday evening.

Miss Money was next seen by a confectioner named Miss Frances Golding, whose shop was at 2 Station Approach, Clapham Junction, where she called to buy some chocolates. She was known to Miss Golding as a customer. She usually called on Wednesdays and Sundays. It was then about seven, so she must have gone straight there. She told Miss Golding that she was going to Victoria. She did not volunteer any further information about herself, and Miss Golding did not ask her.

The remainder of the conversation, which was brief, was confined to the subject of the sweets which Miss Money was purchasing. She was in a merry mood. She left the shop with a laugh, and from that moment until her dead and mutilated body was found in Merstham Tunnel, four hours later, not the smallest clue as to her movements has ever been discovered.

The police admitted interrogating no fewer than 100 persons in connection with the case, but all to no purpose. Scotland Yard, from the Commissioner downwards, took an active interest in the investigation, but could throw no light on it. As usually happens under the circumstances, several persons fell under suspicion, but they were all well able to clear themselves. The coroner's verdict was the familiar and intriguing "open" one.

Let us now take the admitted facts and see what we can make of them.

Miss Money was a young woman of an independent position. She was earning her own living and residing away from home. She was good-looking, had a nice taste in dress, and was just one of those young ladies who would be pretty sure to have plenty of male admirers. Yet, strange to say, much of the evidence seems to point to the fact that she held herself almost entirely aloof from the opposite sex. Certainly her brother mentioned one or two young fellows whom she knew, but they proved to be mere acquaintances. Of evidence of any "love affair" there seemed to be an entire absence.

Her friend, Miss Hone, said she was very reserved, and on Sunday generally sat indoors and wrote. Wrote what? Probably letters to friends. Probably Miss Hone did not know her friend Miss Money so well as she thought she did. For instance, almost immediately after telling Miss Hone she was merely going for a little walk, she told Miss Golding that she was going to Victoria. That is a train journey and not a "little walk". The statement may have been a little fib to cover up her real purpose. One would have felt more satisfied about Miss Money's bona fides if it had been known that she was engaged to or had been engaged to some young man. It is difficult to believe in young and attractive women having no predilection for the opposite sex, or having no friendly intercourse with them.

We may safely accept it that Miss Money did in fact go to Victoria. It seems scarcely likely that she would have any motive in deceiving Miss Golding. She was, however, on a very different footing with Miss Hone. Also a ticket-collector at Clapham Junction identified a photograph of Miss Money as that of a young woman he saw at the station, and who told him that she was going to Victoria.

Although dressed for a walk, she was not equipped for a long journey. Probably she had no intention of going a long journey. What was she doing at Victoria? Probably she went to keep an appointment she had there with a man, with whom she was on cordial terms. She had been, as it is called, "carrying on with him". Sometimes young women of her age consider this "great fun". They really mean nothing, but occasionally the man does not see eye to eye with them. They are playing with fire, although they may not realize it until it is too late. It was a clandestine affair.

What happened after the meeting? One, of course, can only conjecture, basing one's supposition upon the known facts. There is a good deal of time to fill up. They probably strolled about for a while, chatted, had refreshments and so on. Then Miss Money, although she had no real intention of remaining away for very long, may have allowed herself to be persuaded to go for a short run in the train. The refreshment she had had would have the effect of shaking her will-power. What her companion had would merely have strengthened his resolution.

We may imagine the subsequent proceedings thus: The man's object has not yet dawned upon Miss Money. (It need scarcely be pointed out that a first-class railway carriage is a favourite place for a liaison of this kind, especially on a Sunday.) They go a short journey. Possibly to Croydon or London Bridge. The journey is too short to serve the man's purpose. He induces his companion to get into a train going a longer distance. He may have deceived her as to its true destination, may even have represented that it was taking her back home.

On the journey the man's purpose at last becomes obvious to Miss Money, possibly at the same time that she discovers that she is in the wrong train. The adventure reaches a climax. There is a desperate struggle. The woman screams and calls for help. The man is alarmed, tries to silence her, grabs the scarf round her neck, crams it into her mouth. Possibly she faints. The man, half-demented with passion and fear, realizes in a flash the peril of his position. Discovery means ruin to him — he would be charged with a serious crime. He makes a bid for escape. While the train is in the tunnel he opens the door, pitches Miss Money out and recloses the door. At the next stopping-place — Redhill — he makes his escape.

Now, what train did they travel by? On the assumption that the murder occurred within the hour prior to the discovery of the body, there were two trains, either of which would fit the case. These were the 9.33 from Charing Cross, which passed through the tunnel between 10.5 and 10.19, when it was due at Redhill, and the 9.33 from London Bridge to Brighton, which passed through the tunnel at 9.55, and was due at Redhill four minutes later. Either of these trains could have been caught at Croydon.

Some interesting evidence was given by the guard of the train leaving London Bridge. He said that when the train stopped at East Croydon he opened one of the carriage-doors — a first-class carriage, No. 508 — for a passenger, who, however, went into the compartment next to it. At the same time he noticed a man and a woman in the compartment No. 508. The woman was dressed in dark clothes, and wore a "long muslin-looking thing" round her neck. She was young and had a plump face. (Miss Money had a round, plump face.) The man had "a long face and thin chin", and appeared to be fairly tall and powerful. At South Croydon he looked into the carriage again and saw them sitting very close together on the far side, facing the engine. An arm-rest had been pulled up. They were alone in the compartment. He was attracted to them by their behaviour; their movements were suspicious, they appeared to be trying to avoid being seen.

At Redhill the guard saw that the door of compartment 508 was open and the compartment empty. Looking along the platform he saw a man walking towards the exit, whom he believed to be the man he had seen in the carriage sitting by the woman. Unfortunately his description of the man was too vague to be of any practical assistance to the police.

A signalman named Yarnley, stationed in a box at Purley Oaks, had an interesting story to tell. He said that while the train from London Bridge was passing his box he distinctly saw a man and a woman struggling in a first-class carriage. They were standing up, and the man was trying to pull the woman down on the seat. (In this connection it is interesting to recall that in the case of Lefroy, who murdered Mr Gold on the same line some years before, onlookers saw two men standing up and struggling in one of the carriages of the train as it passed.)

The carriages of several trains were closely examined, but no trace of any struggle having taken place in any of them could be discovered.

One may add to this narrative some details of Miss Money's brother, Robert Henry Money, a very curious individual.

He was described as an inveterate liar, and he did, in fact, make so many contradictory statements to the police about his sister's death as to cause them considerable trouble in their efforts to solve the mystery. His subsequent career was about as bad as it could be. He lived a double life of a most odious kind, which eventually culminated in a terrible tragedy. He lived with a woman at Clapham, by whom he had two children. Then he deliberately went away with the woman's sister and married her. By her he had another child. Then he returned to the other woman. He was passing under a false name, the name of Murray, and falsely described himself. He called himself "Captain Murray", but he was in no way connected with the army. He said his father was a barrister, but his father had, in fact, been a carpenter.

This sort of thing went on for some years, until in August 1912, apparently finding himself, or considering himself, at the end of his tether, he conveyed the two women he had alternatively been living with, and the three children, to Eastbourne, where he had taken a furnished house under yet another false name, that of "Mackie". The two women were taken there separately and unknown to each other. He then shot the whole of them dead with the exception of one of the women, who managed to escape from the room, although wounded. He then covered the bodies, which he had placed in one room, with petrol and set light to them, finally shooting himself dead in the same room. When the fire was extinguished, five charred and unrecognizable bodies were found in the room. About £20 in gold was found in a vase and a written message, worded something like this: "I am ruined absolutely, so killed all that are dependent on me. I cannot bear to think that they shall want. Please bury us together. Cannot write any more. God forgive me. C.R. Mackie."

Upon the true identity of "Mackie" and "Murray" being made known, it was significantly hinted that there may have been something more between this wholesale murderer and his sister's murder than was known at the time. This appears doubtful. There was no connection between the two, if you except the partiality both apparently had for clandestine dealings with the opposite sex. It would seem pretty certain that Money had a vicious "kink" in his mental armour, with an incurable predilection for histrionic deception. The solution of the mystery of his unfortunate sister's tragic end may be found in the fact that she also was afflicted with the same dangerous trait.

# The Trial
## of
## John Alexander Dickman

S.O. Rowan-Hamilton

ON FRIDAY, 18 March 1910, a train left Newcastle-upon-Tyne at 10.27 a.m., stopping at all the stations till Alnmouth was reached, where it was due at 12.8 p.m., a distance of $34\frac{3}{4}$ miles. It was quite a short train, consisting of a luggage van and three compartment carriages, and in the one next to the engine John Innes Nisbet was travelling. He was a clerk and a bookkeeper in the employ of the Stobswood Colliery Company, and it was part of his duties to proceed on alternate Fridays to pay the wages at the colliery half a mile away from Widdrington station. The amount of money required varied, but on this occasion he took with him £370 9s. 6d. His employers handed him a cheque, which he cashed at Lloyd's Bank, putting the coin received in canvas bags into a small leather bag, which he locked, retaining the key.

Nisbet was seen by a Mr Charles Raven going in the direction of No. 5 platform, from which the train started, apparently in company with another man whom Raven knew by sight, but not by name. Wilson Hepple, an artist, had taken a seat in the rear of the train, and was walking up and down outside his carriage when he saw John Alexander Dickman, whom he had known for many years, pass with a man, a stranger to him, towards the front part of the train. One of them had his hand on the handle of the compartment, but when he turned round again both had disappeared. Two cashiers, Hall and Spink, were also travelling on the same errand as Nisbet, each to his respective colliery. Hall, on looking out of the window just before the train started, saw Nisbet coming along the platform with a man wearing a light overcoat, and noticed him open the door of the compartment behind theirs and get in, followed by his companion.

On these fortnightly pay journeys it had been the custom of the murdered man's wife to meet her husband on the platform at Heaton, where they lived, and to have a few moments' conversation with him. Heaton is the second station from Newcastle. On this occasion Mrs Nisbet found he was travelling in the front part of the train, whereas he was usually in the rear. Nisbet looked out of the window, but it took her some seconds to reach his compartment. The carriage had stopped under the shadow of a tunnel outside the station, but Mrs Nisbet had just time to observe he was not alone, for she noticed a man was seated at the far end of the carriage, and that the collar of his light overcoat was partly turned up.

The train proceeded on its way to Stannington, at which station the clerks, Hall and Spink, left their carriage, Hall nodding in a friendly way as he passed to Nisbet; they, too, noticed he was not alone. The next station to Stannington is Morpeth, a run of $2\frac{1}{2}$ miles, timed to occupy six minutes. On arrival there, a man gave up to Athey, the ticket collector, the outward half of a return ticket from Newcastle to Stannington and $2\frac{1}{2}$d., which was the correct excess fare. Beyond noticing that he was wearing a loose overcoat, no particular impression was made on Athey. During the time the train stopped at Morpeth to take up water — a matter of about four minutes — a passenger named Grant, trying to find a comfortable seat, looked casually into the third compartment of the first carriage, which was apparently empty, and passed on.

When the train arrived at Alnmouth, the foreman porter, William Charlton, on opening the door of the third compartment in the first carriage, made a gruesome discovery. From under the seat came three streams of blood, and on his bending down he discovered the body of a man lying face downwards and pushed as far back as possible. Examination showed the unfortunate person had been shot in no less than five places in the head. A broken pair of spectacles proved that life had not been surrendered without a struggle.

A hard felt hat on the floor of the carriage led to the identification of the deceased as James Nisbet. A post-mortem examination disclosed that two out of the five bullets were still lodged in his head; one was an ordinary lead bullet, but the other was nickel-capped. As they were of different calibre, it seemed clear that the murderer had needed two revolvers to accomplish his foul work.

*The Trial of John Alexander Dickman*

A reward of £100 was at once offered by the employers of
the murdered man:

£100 REWARD.

MURDER

Whereas on the 17th March, 1910, John Innes Nisbet, a clerk or
cashier, late of 180 Heaton Road, Newcastle, was murdered in a
third-class carriage on the North-Eastern Railway between Newcastle and Alnmouth, and a black leather bag containing £370 9s.
6d. in money (mostly gold and silver), which was in charge of the
deceased man, was stolen.

A man of the following description was seen in the same carriage
as the deceased at Newcastle and Stannington railway stations, and
appeared to be on friendly terms with the deceased:- About
thirty-five to forty years of age, about 5 feet 6 inches high, about 11
stones in weight, medium build; heavy, dark moustache, pale or
sallow complexion; wore a light overcoat, down to his knees; black,
hard, felt hat; well dressed and appeared to be fairly well to do.

The above reward will be paid by the owners of the Stobswood
Colliery, near Widdrington, to any person (other than a person
belonging to the police force in the United Kingdom), not being the
actual murderer, who shall be the first to give such information and
shall give such evidence as shall lead to the discovery and the
conviction of the murderer or murderers.

Rumour, as usual, was not silent; the murderer had been
seen in many places, and in London had offered a drink to a
busman, showing him at the same time a handful of gold.
With surprising swiftness the man was traced, but, promptly
proving his right to the money, he was equally promptly
discharged.

Information, however, reached the police that John
Dickman had been in the company of the deceased, and
Detective Inspector Tait called at his house in the Jesmond
district of Newcastle. He was not cautioned, nor can one
gather that he was at the time looked upon other than as a
witness whose evidence might be useful to the police. After
some conversation Dickman told the inspector he had seen
Nisbet on the morning of the murder, had booked his ticket at
the same time, had travelled by the same train, but had not
seen him after the train started, as he did not travel in the same

73

compartment. Asked if he would make a statement at the police office, he at once acquiesced, and accompanied by the inspector went there and made a voluntary statement which was written down, read over to him, and signed by him as correct.

The statement described his movements at the station on the morning of 18 March — how he travelled in a carriage at the end of the train, passed Stannington station without noticing it and got out at Morpeth, paying an excess fare of $2\frac{1}{2}$d.; after starting to walk back to Stannington he was taken ill and returned to Morpeth to catch the 1.12 p.m. train back to Newcastle. This he missed, but took the 1.40 train instead. While waiting for this train he left the station, walking towards the town, meeting a man called Elliott, with whom he conversed for a few moments. In conclusion, he said that the object of his journey was to see a Mr Hogg at Dovecot Colliery.

As the statement was in contradiction to evidence already in the possession of the police, Dickman was at once arrested.

The police visited his house, and found in a bureau some pawn tickets for small articles pawned in the name of "John Wilkinson", one of which was pawned the day before the murder. In the same bureau were also found a life preserver and two pass-books, one relating to an account at the National Provincial Bank and the other to an account at Lambton's (since amalgamated with Lloyds). Amongst the clothing seized by the police were a pair of trousers with a pair of suede gloves, which were found to have bloodstains on them. No revolvers were — or ever have been — discovered.

The question of the identification of the prisoner was of vital importance, both to the prosecution and to the defence. From the very first, perhaps it is not too much to say that it became the only question; and it becomes necessary to see how and by what means the links in the chain of identification are connected, and especially to notice two incidents which did not come to light at the trial, but which were subsequently discovered.

As Dickman admitted he was at the station on the 18th and

had travelled by the 10.27 a.m. train, there is no need to consider the evidence as to that fact. But it is necessary to consider the statements of the witnesses for the prosecution, contrasting their story with his own.

The first evidence on this question was given by Charles Raven, who knew the prisoner by sight but not by name, and who knew Nisbet quite well. He saw them enter the platform together, but did not hear them conversing.

The artist Hepple knew Dickman intimately, but did not know Nisbet. He saw Dickman on the platform with somebody, but his evidence carries the case no further on this point. He also saw one of them with his hand on the handle of a carriage door while he was walking up and down outside his own compartment, and on looking round later noticed they had presumably entered the carriage together, as they were no longer on the platform.

Now, the witness Hall knew Nisbet, but not the prisoner, not even by sight. He identified Nisbet as being the person who opened the carriage door; though he only saw his companion for two or three seconds, he was quite close to him and "got a fairly good view". On 21 March, at the police station, he was taken to a room in which nine men were placed, from whom he was asked to identify the prisoner. He picked Dickman out, at the same time saying, "If I was assured that the murderer was in amongst those nine men, I would have no hesitation in picking the prisoner out" — not very strong identification at the best, but hardly identification at all in view of what has transpired subsequently.

The suspicion of the leading counsel for the defence was aroused at the trial by this answer, but nothing definite was elicited. But between the verdict and the appeal to the Court of Criminal Appeal these suspicions became confirmed, as was shown by a letter from the chief constable of Northumberland to the Under-Secretary of State at the Home Office. From this it appears that when Hall and Spink went to identify Dickman at the police station, while waiting in a corridor it was suggested to them by a constable that they should look through a window of a room in which Dickman was being examined, to see if they could recognize him before being officially asked to do so. They both went to the window, but owing to the lower part being frosted, they could only see the top of a man's head, and consequently declined to draw the deduction that he was the man they had seen in the train with Nisbet. Another attempt was then made by the police to facilitate the identification through a half-open door, and this time Hall noticed the light overcoat Dickman was wearing, and was therefore in a better position to identify him from the other nine men. It would be interesting to know if all these, or any of them, at the time Hall was called upon officially to identify Dickman, were wearing similar overcoats.

Why should the officers have suggested to Hall and Spink this illegal and underhand means of identification, not a word of which was mentioned at the trial? It is to be feared that much of the so-called identification that takes place at police stations is of a similar, wrongful, and unfair description.

Let me now pass on to the second incident in the identification of the prisoner.

Mrs Nisbet was called before the magistrates, and first gave evidence on 14 April. She spoke of seeing her husband in the train and running along the platform to his carriage, and then, a fainting attack coming on, it was some time before she could resume. She again swooned at the close of her evidence. Other evidence was called, and the prisoner was remanded till the 22nd, on which date Mrs Nisbet expressed her desire to make a further statement, which was as follows: "The little I saw of the man in the train that morning, he had his coat collar up and it partly covered his face. I recognized the same part of his face in the dock the other day, and that is how I lost my senses...."

It never transpired till after the trial that Mrs Nisbet had known Dickman by sight for years, and remembered seeing him only shortly before the murder. It would have been better if she had returned into court on the 14th and made her statement then, rather than postpone it for days — till the 22nd — when she must have had every opportunity of talking it over with the police and others. One would have thought she would have returned to the court, and then and there denounced Dickman. Her excuse for delay is that she "was not called upon to do so". Surely after such a startling incident this would have suggested itself even to the lay mind!

But does not the fact that Mrs Nisbet failed to recognize at once a man she had known for years throw a grave suspicion on the value not only of her identification of Dickman, but on every particle of her evidence? Why under the circumstances should she have hesitated so long before she became convinced of his identity?

The murder, it must not be forgotten, was undoubtedly committed between Stannington and Morpeth. The evidence of Grant, who looked into the carriage occupied by Nisbet and found it apparently empty at Morpeth, and the evidence of officials along the line, disposes of any other premise. The last witness as to the identification was Athey, the ticket collector, who declined to say more than that Dickman resembled in his general appearance the man who left the train at Morpeth.

It now becomes necessary to consider the question as to the possession of firearms by the prisoner; nor must it be forgotten that no firearms were found at his house, nor have the revolvers* with which the crime was perpetrated ever been discovered. Dickman was in the habit of having letters sent to him, under the name of "F. Black", at a place of business in Newcastle kept by a Miss Hymen. Many of the letters were concerned with betting transactions, but undoubtedly about the end of October a small parcel was

---

* Although I have treated the evidence as pointing to two pistols being used in the murder, there is little doubt that one only was employed. The murderer had endeavoured to make the small bullets fit the barrel by wrapping paper round the cartridge. In this he was only partially successful, which accounts for the loss of penetrative power as referred to in the evidence. One such piece of paper was found in the carriage, but it was not realized to what use it had been put. The prosecution, having to account for the bullets of different calibre, naturally formed the conclusion that two revolvers had been employed. There is now no doubt that only one was used. My authority for this statement is Mr Mitchell-Innes, K.C. (who was the leading counsel for the defence).

delivered from a firm of gunsmiths, addressed to him under his pseudonym. Dickman did not call for it for a couple of months, and in the meantime a postcard was received for him from the firm, asking for the return of the revolver sent in error. This postcard was read by the proprietress of the shop, who when he called in January 1910, gave him a label for the purpose of returning it; but she had no knowledge whether in fact he had done so, as he took both parcel and label away with him. This was the last time he was in Miss Hymen's shop, and on that occasion, for some reason known only to himself, he told her his correct name was Dickman and gave his address.

The evidence of the gunsmith on behalf of the prosecution shows that two of the four bullets produced were such as are used in an automatic pistol; but no evidence was presented that Dickman possessed another revolver.

The medical evidence was given by Dr Boland, who conducted the post-mortem and examined the bloodstains on Dickman's left-hand glove and the left pocket of his trousers; he declined to decide whether it was the blood of a human being or even of a mammal, but was positive as to the stains not being more than a fortnight old when he examined them on 26 March. On the outside of the prisoner's overcoat he discovered a large dark stain on the left front, and microscopical examination showed that efforts had been made to remove it by means of an oil (probably paraffin); but of what nature the stain was Dr Boland could give no opinion, owing to the action of the oil.

On 9 June, about a month before the trial, an important discovery was made. Peter Spooner, a colliery manager at the Hepcott colliery, found at the bottom of an air shaft at the Isabella pit the bag Nisbet was carrying with him when he was murdered. The Isabella mine is $1\frac{1}{4}$ miles south-east of Morpeth station, close to the high road. Dickman was an acquaintance of Spooner, and the latter had spoken to him on certain occasions as to the difficulty of working this pit owing to the large quantity of water. The air shaft was covered by an iron grid with bars 6 inches or $6\frac{1}{2}$ inches apart, sufficiently wide to admit the passage of the bag; the grid could also be lifted quite easily. This air shaft was only visited occasionally, about once in five weeks.

The bag, which was locked, had a large cut in the side, and the contents were missing, with the exception of a few coppers, while round the place where it lay other coppers were scattered.

The motive of the murder obviously being robbery, it becomes necessary to inquire into the prisoner's financial condition.

Dickman, after he had given up the secretaryship of a colliery syndicate, worked on a variable commission with certain bookmakers, and at one time had an office in Newcastle. He kept two banking accounts, one at Lambton's, which was closed in December 1909, and only small sums had ever been passed through it. The other account was at the National and Provincial Bank.

In October 1909, he borrowed £20 for three months at 60 per cent per annum from the Cash Accommodation and Investment Company, which high-toned name covers the dealing of an ordinary moneylending business. The sum was payable on demand, with interest at £1 per month. In the following January, 1910, though the interest had been paid regularly, Dickman called at the office and obtained an extension of the loan for a further period of three months, on the ground that he was not in a position to repay the principal. This interest was carefully paid, the last payment being made on 17 March — the day before the murder.

In November 1909, Dickman introduced to the company a Mr Frank Christie, who obtained a loan from them of £200. The whole of this sum found its way at once into Dickman's account at the National and Provincial Bank, but found its way out again directly, Dickman withdrawing it on the 26th and 29th of the same month by cheques payable to himself. Mr Christie gave evidence that of the £200, he eventually received about half. Other large amounts had from time to time been paid to Dickman's account, but no transaction took place after this last-mentioned cheque was presented for payment.

On 14 February 1910, Dickman again appears to have been in low water, for he visited a firm styling themselves Cush & Co., jewellers, of Newcastle, and obtained £5 on the security of some jewellery of trifling value. He stated to Mr Kettering, a partner, that he required the money to go to Liverpool to see the Waterloo Cup race. A few days later, meeting another of the partners, he expressed his desire to repay the loan shortly, regretting he was unable to do so at the moment.

This being the state of his financial resources, let us see if Mrs Dickman was in a position to help him.

In January 1910, she had a sum of about £15 standing to her credit, but practically the whole of it was withdrawn by the middle of February. In addition, she had an account at a Co-operative society; this showed a credit in 1907 of roughly £73, but had by March 1910 fallen to £4. In January 1910, she wrote from Newcastle to her husband, who was away at the time:

> Dear Jack,
> I received your card, and am sorry that you have no money to send. I am needing it very badly. The weather here is past description. I had to get in a load of coals, which consumed the greater part of a sovereign. The final notice for rates has come in — in fact, came in last week — which means they must be paid next Thursday. Also Harry's school account. With my dividend due this week and what is in the Post Office I dare say I can pay the most pressing things, but it is going to make the question of living a poser, unless you can give me some advice as to what to do....
> Trusting to hear from you soon regarding what you think I had best do,
>
> I am,
> Yours faithfully,
> Annie Dickman

So in January Mrs Dickman is engaged in a fruitless endeavour to obtain from her husband the necessities of life. At the time she wrote that letter, she had the sum of £32 to her credit. But she foresaw that with her husband earning nothing, relying very largely on the uncertainty of backing the winning horse, the "question of living" was rapidly becoming "a poser". Although Dickman had in the previous November obtained a sum of something over £100 from Mr Christie, it did not satisfy his requirements for very long, for in December he journeyed to Stannington to try to borrow a couple of pounds from Hogg to "tide him over", and it will be remembered that it was in the following January he was asking for an extension of the loan from the Investment Company through Cohen, a moneylender, and in February had been obliged to pawn jewellery to raise a five-pound note. On the day before the murder their united funds amounted to a sum of £4 — and as to this, it is not certain whether Dickman even knew of its existence. Mrs Dickman, like many other wise women, doubtless endeavoured to get as much money out of her husband as the occasion allowed, and to put away in her own name all she could spare for a "rainy day".

In his cross-examination Dickman said, "We had some little bickering as to who should pay or draw upon certain things at the time, but, however, I gave way and settled matters."

At any rate, on 17 March their financial position must have been acute, if not critical. There was ample motive, if such were possible, for Dickman to commit the crime.

On 21 March, when Dickman was arrested, the sum of £17 9s. 11d. was found on him in coin in one of Lambton & Co.'s small bags. Owing to the amalgamation of Lloyds with Lambton's, the clerk in their employ could not say in whose bags the £370 9s. 6d. was originally put.

Neither the weapons with which the deed was perpetrated nor the bulk of the money were ever found. The murderer — whether Dickman or some other man — laid his plans well, and with a care that showed the most thorough premeditation; notwithstanding the closest search, no trace of the cash beyond the coppers in the Isabella pit was discovered. Did he hide the money, intending to come for the spoil some future day? If Dickman was rightly convicted of the crime, the secret of his hiding-place was well kept, as indeed it will be, for it lies with him at the bottom of a nameless grave.

In 1898 an Act of Parliament was passed which has been, perhaps, more far-reaching in its effects on the criminal law than any other statute. By the first section of the Act, the accused person and the wife or husband of the accused may give evidence for the defence. He or she cannot be called upon to do so; it is entirely a voluntary matter. It is expressly laid down that should they decide not to avail themselves of the privilege, the opposing counsel may not comment on their absence from the witness-box. This last clause became of importance later.

In a case of so mysterious a character, a case that created such an immense amount of interest, it is a little curious that the only witness called for the defence was the prisoner himself. He availed himself of the Act allowing him to give evidence, and faced what must have been a severe ordeal with the same composure as he had exhibited throughout the proceedings.

In answer to questions of his counsel, he stated that his visits to the witness Hogg were never by appointment, that he saw Nisbet on the morning of 18 March, that his acquaintance with the deceased was of a casual nature only, and that he never saw Nisbet after leaving the ticket office, where he had taken his ticket to Stannington. It being the morning of the Grand National, the racing news was of special interest, so he bought a *Manchester Sporting Chronicle* to study the latest stable information while *en route*. The swerve on the railway between Stannington and Morpeth brought him back to reality, and he realized that he had passed his station. He left the train at Morpeth, paying the excess fare. He was carrying his overcoat over his arm or shoulder.

It would perhaps be advisable to leave for a moment Dickman's evidence and glance at the accompanying map. It will be seen that there are two roads leading from Morpeth station to Stannington, one the main road to Newcastle, the other, to the east of the railway, joining the main road near Stannington station. The direct route from Morpeth station to the Dovecot Moor Colliery (where Hogg was engaged) would have been along the high road.

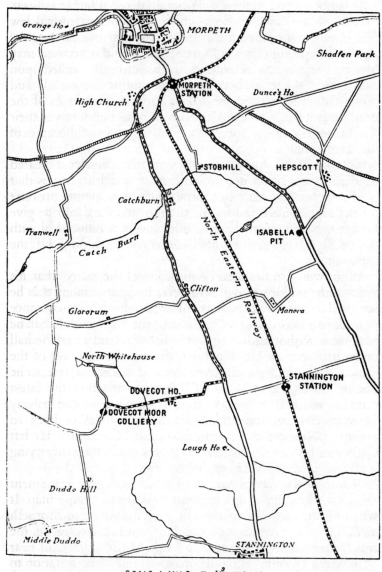

SCALE 1 MILE = $1\frac{9}{32}$ INCHES

Returning to his evidence: Dickman decided not to go back to Stannington by the train, which he knew left Morpeth a few minutes later, because if he had carried out his original plans, after seeing Hogg at Dovecot, he would have walked to Morpeth station, as he wished to inspect the Landsale Drift, past which the road between these station leads. So after leaving Morpeth station, he had walked for about half an hour until he reached a village known to him as Clifton, where he was taken ill and was forced to lie down in an adjoining field for about half an hour; but one must confess that the symptoms of his complaint are somewhat mysterious. This sudden indisposition decided Dickman to return at once to Newcastle, and he reached Morpeth station a few minutes late for the express. As he had some time to wait for the next train, he left the station on the east side, and met Elliot, who was with a friend. He then returned alone and took the 1.45 p.m. train home.

With regard to the parcel, which it was alleged contained a revolver from Messrs Bell Brothers, Dickman stated that he returned it unopened and was not aware of its contents.

Dickman was then examined as to his financial affairs, and gave evidence contradicting much that was tendered on behalf of the prosecution. He stated that the canvas bag in which the money was found was his own and that he used it as a purse. But he affirmed that he had £120 in reserve known only to himself, with part of which sum he intended to start betting when the flat-race season opened. This £120 was intact in the previous November, and out of this some time before Christmas he gave his wife £50. It was made up partly of his own and partly of Mr Frank Christie's money. By the middle of February £40 remained, all of which was his own. It had been his intention to go to see the Waterloo Cup run, but when he abandoned that idea, he gave his wife a further £15 or £20. The £17 which was found on him at the police station was the remainder of the reserve fund of £120.

In cross-examination, Dickman agreed that he was an ex-secretary to a colliery company, and that he knew colliery wages in the district were paid on alternate Fridays. He admitted making the journey on 4 March, also a Friday, stating he wished to see Hogg with regard to the payment of wages, though he had no appointment with him, and no interest in the sinking operations at Dovecot. "*Q.* How long before that did you visit Mr Hogg? — That I could not say. *Q.* Was it usually on a Friday? — It might have been; I think it was."

These frequent journeys on a Friday — what was their object? His desire (exposed under cross-examination as to the financial operations between Hogg and Christie) to find out whether Christie was "bluffing" when he told him he had no money: was this the real object? Or was there a deeper motive, necessitating a careful reconnaissance of the ground, a practical demonstration of the noise made by the train at the fastest portion of the track, assessment of the distance between Stannington and Morpeth? Was the story of Mr Brocklehurst and his companions,* though no evidence against the prisoner, altogether devoid of foundation?

Dickman maintained that on the day in question he was wearing an old brown overcoat, not the fawn-coloured "Burberry", as described by the witnesses for the prosecution, and he produced both in the box.

There were others, he said, travelling in the same compartment with him, possibly five or six, but he paid no

---

* From the *Newcastle Daily Chronicle*, 22 March 1910:
  Mr A.G. Brocklehurst, 57 Tavistock Road, Jesmond, Newcastle, a commercial traveller, in an interview with one of our reporters yesterday, said that about a fortnight ago he and several others were travelling by the 9.30 express from Newcastle to Morpeth, when between Annitsford and Stannington they were startled by a noise that sounded like revolver shooting. On letting down the carriage window and looking out they saw that the framework outside the window of their compartment was splintered, apparently by bullets fired from a revolver by a person in another compartment. Mr Brocklehurst and his companions were travelling in the last compartment in the second carriage from the engine. Had the shots been fired from the outside of the train they would have gone into the compartment instead of glancing off.

attention to them, hardly observing whether they were men or women. The surprise caused by the shock of his arrest and the accusation launched against him had driven from his mind all thoughts and all details of his fellow passengers on that eventful morning.

The visit to Mr Hogg was not the only object of the journey, for a Mr Houldsworth had consulted him as to the value of the Landsale Drift. When asked why he did not return from Morpeth to Stannington by the train due in a few minutes, he replied, "If I had got out at Stannington I should have gone to the Dovecot pit, and then I should have walked from the Dovecot pit to Morpeth; by walking back from Morpeth to the Dovecot pit I should pass the Landsale Drift — so I was merely stopping, as it were, at the wrong end of the journey."

He adhered to the details of his attack of illness on the road (during his detention he was attended for the same complaint). Obviously it was not a very serious affair, as on reaching home he went out after tea.

Of the position and features of the Isabella Pit he denied all knowledge, though he might "have passed it and not known". Peter Spooner he knew to be connected with the Hepscott Colliery on the east side of Morpeth station.

The suede gloves on which the bloodstains were found had been discarded some three months before; they fitted badly, and were thrown aside. How the bloodstains had got on them he could give no account, unless his nose had bled, or he had at some time or other received a cut and touched the place with them. In spite of the evidence of the analyst, who deposed that the bloodstains were of recent date, he maintained that he had neither worn nor carried the gloves since Christmas. The blood-marks on the inside of the trouser pocket probably came from the same cause — with the addition of a new source: perhaps when "he was cutting his corns". The oil on his coat came from his bicycle.

He denied that he required any money in October, and stated that he went to Cohen to "ascertain if it were possible to obtain loans at the advertised rate of interest, and for no other purpose". He asserted that in February he had a sum of £70, but could not repay Cohen the borrowed £20.

Asked to explain attempts to borrow money from Swinney (a witness not called at the trial) and from Hogg, he answered that with regard to Swinney he did not want to borrow for himself, and with regard to the loan by Hogg it was to save him the trouble of going home.

As for the jeweller Kettering's evidence that he was pawning goods, he declined to look at it in that light, describing the transaction as merely "putting them in a place of safety", because of the recent burglaries in the neighbourhood. The use of the name John Wilkinson "was an idea of a moment".

These answers, especially as to his transactions with Cohen, must have raised the gravest suspicion in the minds of the jury as to the truth of his whole story. Is it possible that a fairly well-educated person, who had held a responsible position, would borrow money at 60 per cent interest just to find out if the moneylender's advertisements were true? Neither could his story with regard to the £5 borrowed from Kettering's company be regarded by reasonable men as other than an invention. These are merely two of the improbabilities that occurred in his narrative.

In the course of his address to the jury, Mr Tindal Atkinson, leading counsel for the Crown, inadvertently commented on the fact that Mrs Dickman had not been called by the defence to give certain evidence on behalf of her husband as to matters which must have been within her knowledge. Such comment is in contradiction with the express terms of the statute mentioned above. The defence were placed in a difficulty. If Mr Mitchell-Innes at once objected, however rapidly he did so, he could not have prevented the jury knowing that he could have called evidence on certain points, which he had thought wiser to keep in the background. If he took no objection, he might then hope that on this ground the Court of Criminal Appeal would quash the conviction, though it might have been said that objection ought to have been taken at the trial.

During his speech for the defence, Mr Mitchell-Innes alluded to the incident, and Mr Tindal Atkinson apologized, saying that the comment was made "in pure inadvertence and forgetfulness of the extent of the provisions in the Act of Parliament".

The jury retired a few minutes before one, returning about two and a half hours later. Before the verdict was given, the judge, Lord Coleridge, who had not referred to the incident of the inadvertent comment during his summing-up, sought to remedy the omission:

> Such comment is forbidden, I ought to have said, but it escaped my attention for the moment.... [It] ought to be banished from your minds, and not to influence your verdict. If you have allowed that comment to affect your minds adversely to the prisoner, I must ask you to reconsider your verdict, dismissing such comment from your minds. If you have not allowed it to affect your decision in any way, then you can deliver your verdict.
> The Foreman (without consulting the other jurymen) — It has not.
> Lord Coleridge — Have you allowed it to affect you?
> The Foreman — We have not.
> Lord Coleridge — Then that question does not arise.
> The Foreman — It has not been mentioned.
> Lord Coleridge — I understand you have not allowed it to affect your minds.
> The Foreman — We have not mentioned it.

The verdict of "Guilty" was then delivered.

Asked if he had anything to say, Dickman, in calm, clear tones, reiterated his innocence. "I can only repeat that I am entirely innocent of this cruel deed. I have no complicity in this crime, and I have spoken the truth in my evidence — in everything that I have said."

Sentence of death was then passed by Lord Coleridge:

> Prisoner at the bar, the patient, careful trial is now ended, the irrevocable decision has now been given. The jury have found you guilty of murder. In your hungry lust for gold you had no pity upon the victim whom you slew, and it is only just that the nemesis of the law should overtake the author of the crime. The scales of justice are now balanced by the verdict which your fellows have pronounced. The punishment is death.

There is a silence that creeps round a court of justice while the sentence of death is being pronounced. Just for a few seconds it seems as if the noise of the world is hushed, and time stands still. Each hears his own heart beat; the crowded gallery strain and crane their necks to get a look at the man who is holding on to the rail, with a warder on each side. His friends sob audibly; tears stream from the eyes of the women who have cared for him, with all his faults; sometimes a wife or lover faints. Hardly a soul does not feel an instant's terror when the Spirit of Death stalks in to claim his prize.

"I declare," said Dickman, turning round, "I declare to all men, I am innocent."

Many efforts were made to save the condemned man. The Court of Criminal Appeal, not very long established, declined to interfere. A petition for a reprieve, very largely signed, was forwarded to the Home Secretary. Even his refusal to interfere did not bring the efforts of Dickman's friends to a close, for on the day before his execution London was flooded with handbills bearing in huge type the following words:

Must Dickman be hanged to-morrow? No! No! No!
Wire Home Secretary at once and wash your hands of complicity in the legal crime.

These were left at nearly every restaurant and public-house and were distributed in the streets by both men and women of every rank and calling in society. Circulars to the same effect were sent out all over the country and hundreds of telegrams and letters endeavoured unsuccessfully to obtain from the Home Office a respite of the sentence.

John Alexander Dickman died within the precincts of Newcastle prison on 10 August 1910.

# S.O. Rowan-Hamilton

## Postscript

MEMORANDUM SUBMITTED TO THE ROYAL COMMISSION ON CAPITAL
PUNISHMENT, 1949-53, CHAIRED BY SIR ERNEST GOWERS:

This subject has interested me for many years, particularly
since the trial of Rex *v.* Dickman at the Newcastle Summer
Assizes in July 1910, who was tried for the murder of a man
named Nesbit [sic] in a train. Dickman was executed for what
was an atrocious crime on 10 August 1910, his appeal to the
Court of Criminal Appeal being dismissed on 22 July 1910.
The case has always troubled me and converted me into an
opponent of capital punishment. I attended the trial as the
acting official shorthand-writer under the Criminal Appeal
Act. I took a different view to the jury; I thought the case was
not conclusively made out against the accused. Singularly
enough, in view of the nature of the crime, five of the jurymen
signed the petition for reprieve, which could only be based
upon the notion that the evidence was not sufficient against
the accused.

It may be asked, why raise the question now? I am doing so
partly because of Viscount Templewood's evidence when he
was reported as saying there was a possibility of innocent men
being executed: partly because of the evidence of Viscount
Buckmaster before the Barr Committee on Capital Punishment; but mainly because of the remarkable and disturbing
matters concerning the Dickman case which have come to my
knowledge over the intervening years, which I will now relate.

The Dickman case is the subject of a book by Sir S.
Rowan-Hamilton, which was published in 1914, based on the
transcripts of the shorthand notes of the trial and certain other
material. I did not read this book till August 1939, when,
owing to certain passages in the book, I wrote a letter to Sir S.
Rowan-Hamilton, who had been Chief Justice of Bermuda,
who replied as follows in a letter dated 26 October 1939:

The Cottage,
Craijavak,
Co. Down.

Sir,

Your interesting letter of the 24th August only reached me to-day. Of course, I was not present at the incident you referred to in the Judge's Chamber's, but (Charles) Lowenthal (junior Crown counsel at Dickman's trial) was a fierce prosecutor. All the same Dickman was justly (convicted?), and it may interest you to know that he was with little doubt the murderer of Mrs Luard [who was shot dead at Ightham, near Sevenoaks, Kent, on 24 August 1908], for he had forged a cheque she had sent him in response to an advertisement in *The Times* (I believe) asking for help; she discovered it and wrote to him and met him outside the General's and her house and her body was found there. He was absent from Newcastle those exact days. Tindal Atkinson knew of this, but not being absolutely certain, refused to cross-examine Dickman on it. I have seen replicas of cheques. They were shown me by the Public Prosecutor.... He was, I believe, mixed up in that case, but I have forgotten the details.

Yours very truly,
S. Rowan-Hamilton, Kt.

In 1938 there was published a book entitled *Great Unsolved Crimes*, by various authors. In that book there is an article by ex-Superintendent Percy Savage (who was in charge of the investigations), entitled "The Fish Ponds Wood Mystery", which deals with the murder of Mrs Luard, wife of Major-General Luard, who committed suicide shortly afterwards by putting himself on the railway line. In that article the following passage appears: "It remains an unsolved mystery. All our work was in vain. The murderer was never caught, as not a scrap of evidence was forthcoming on which we could justify an arrest, and, to this day, I frankly admit that I have no idea who the criminal was." This book first came to my notice in February 1949, whereupon I wrote to Sir Rowan-Hamilton, reminding him of the previous letters, and asking for his observations on this statement of the officer who had conducted the inquiries into the Luard case. On 22 February 1949, I received the following reply from Sir S. Rowan-Hamilton:

Lisieux,
Sandycove Road,
Dunloaoghaire,
Co. Dublin.

*22nd February, 1949.*

Dear Sir,

Thank you for your letter. Superintendent Savage was certainly
not at Counsel's conference and so doubtless knew nothing of what
passed between them. I am keeping your note as you are interested
in the case and will send you later a note on the Luard case.

Yours truly,
S. Rowan-Hamilton, Kt.

I replied, pointing out what a disturbing state of facts was
revealed, as it was within my knowledge that Lord Coleridge,
who tried Dickman, Lord Alverstone, Mr Justice A.T.
Lawrence, and Mr Justice Phillimore, who constituted the
Court of Criminal Appeal, were friends of Major-General and
Mrs Luard. (Lord Alverstone made a public statement
denouncing in strong language the conduct of certain people
who had written anonymous letters to Major-General Luard
hinting that he had murdered his wife.) I did not receive any
reply to this letter, nor the promised note on the Luard case.

Mr Winston Churchill, who was the Home Secretary who
rejected all representations on behalf of Dickman, was also a
friend of Major-General Luard.

So one has the astonishing state of things disclosed that
Dickman was tried for the murder of Nesbit [sic] by judges
who already had formed the view that he was guilty of the
murder of the wife of a friend of theirs. If Superintendent
Savage is to be believed, this was an entirely mistaken view.

I was surprised at the time of the trial at the venom which
was displayed towards the prisoner by those in charge of the
case. When I was called in to Lord Coleridge's room to read
my note before the verdict was given on the point of the
non-calling of Mrs Dickman as a witness, I was amazed to find
in the judge's room Mr Lowenthal, Junior Counsel for the
Crown, the police officers in charge of the case, and the
solicitor for the prosecution. When I mentioned this in a

subsequent interview with Lord Alverstone, he said I must not refer to the matter in view of my official position.

I did my best at the time within the limits possible. I went to Mr Burns, the only Cabinet-Minister I knew well, and told him my views on the case and the incident in the judge's room; which I also told to Mr Gardiner, the Editor of *The Daily News*, who said he could not refer to that, though he permitted me to write in his room a last-day appeal for a reprieve, which appeared in *The Daily News*. Mr John Burns told me afterwards that he had conveyed my representations to Mr Churchill, but without avail.

C.H. NORMAN,
*27 November 1950*

# The Killing
## of
# Willie Starchfield

Richard Whittington-Egan

IN THE gathering twilight of a January afternoon, a train of the old North London Railway was smokily chugging its way through a grey townscape of soot-stained churches, seedy public-houses, and acres of regimented Victorian dwelling-houses that unwound in desolate dreariness between Chalk Farm and Broad Street stations. As it wheezed to a stop at Mildmay Park, sixteen-year-old George Tillman, a cabinet-maker's apprentice, clambered into what he thought was an empty compartment.

A minute or two later, noticing that his bootlace had come undone, he bent down to tie it — and saw something that set the hair bristling on the back of his neck. There, under the opposite seat, was a small, bare knee … and two wax-white, deathly-still hands.

Frightened, the lad sat like a statue until the next stop — Dalston — where he catapulted out onto the murky platform and tried unsuccessfully to attract the attention of the guard. It was not until he reached his destination, Haggerston, that young Tillman managed to find a railway official and tell him of his gruesome discovery.

By then the train had lurched on, but the Haggerston stationmaster's telephone call to Shoreditch sent a porter there scurrying to meet it.

And, sure enough, crumpled up in the dust under the seat, he found the strangled body of a small, curly-haired boy. The time was 4.32 p.m. The date: 8 January 1914.

*At that time* … two women were frantically scouring the teeming London streets for a missing child. He was five-year-old Willie Starchfield. That morning, his mother, Mrs Agnes Starchfield, an out-of-work tailoress, had left him in the care of Mrs Emily Longstaff, the landlady of her lodgings at 191 Hampstead Road, Camden, while she went

*Willie Starchfield*

out to look for work.

Willie had last been seen shortly after half-past twelve, when Mrs Longstaff had sent him on an errand to a stationer's shop just down the road. He had still not returned when his mother came home at 3 p.m. Willie was Agnes Starchfield's only surviving child — two had died — and he was delicate. He had long, light brown curls, like a girl's.

*At that time* ... John Starchfield, Willie's father and Agnes's thirty-five-year-old, separated husband, was selling newspapers at his pitch on the corner of Oxford Street and Tottenham Court Road, as, apart from a stint in the King's Royal Rifles, he had been doing for sixteen years.

His moment of glory had come on 27 September 1912, when a mad Armenian tailor, Stephen Titus, had run amok with a revolver in the bar of the Horseshoe Hotel, Tottenham Court Road, and killed the manageress. As Titus came hurtling out into the street, Starchfield tackled and captured him. For this act of heroism he received a near-fatal bullet in the stomach and a pound-a-week award from the Carnegie Hero Fund.

As a husband, he cut a less heroic figure. He had been twice imprisoned for failure to maintain his wife. Now, his Carnegie pound was paid direct to her — and he was living alone in a common lodging-house in Long Acre. Very soon the estranged husband and wife were to be tragically brought together by the pathetic little body lying in Shoreditch Mortuary.

It did not take the police long to establish that the murdered boy was indeed little Willie Starchfield. The medical evidence indicated the time of death as between 2 and 3 p.m., but there was nothing to show whether the boy had been actually killed in the train, or placed there already dead.

By midnight, the police were interviewing John Starchfield. He exhibited little emotion when told of his son's murder. He had not been in the Camden neighbourhood that afternoon, he said, and he could prove it, because he had stayed in bed until 3.30 p.m. at the lodging-house, feeling ill with his old bullet wound. Another lodger, William Tilley, slept in the same six-bedded room, and had been there with him until 3 p.m.

There was already much public interest by the time the inquest opened on 15 January, and the police had been industrious in their enquiries. A possible "murder weapon" had been found on 9 January by Joseph Rodgers, a signalman, who picked up on the railway track near Broad Street Station a yard-length of blind-cord, tied up in a bow. Dr Bernard Spilsbury, the pathologist, thought it could have been the cord used to strangle the boy.

There was even an eye-witness of what might have been the murder scene. George Robert Jackson, a signalman stationed at the St. Pancras box, half-way between Camden Town and Maiden Lane stations, said he saw a man with a dark moustache and a dark coat leaning over the form of someone who had fair, curly hair. He thought at first it was a girl. The time would have been about 2.07 p.m.

John Starchfield had a dark moustache, compelling eyes and a rather Italian appearance, and it became obvious that, so far as the police were concerned, he was a prime suspect.

A vitally important witness was Mrs Clara Wood. It was she who provided the clue of the coconut cake. At 1.15 p.m. on 8 January, she was shopping in Kentish Town Road and, just by the corner of Angler's Lane, saw a dark, Italian-looking man, with a heavy, dark moustache, leading a boy of about five, with thick, brown curly hair. The boy was munching a cake, and as he passed, Mrs Wood, her maternal heart moved, murmured, "Oh, bless it!"

It was only when she saw in the newspaper that Dr Spilsbury's analysis of the murdered boy's stomach-content included cake that she reported the incident to the police. Then, turning detective, she produced a coconut cake which she had specially bought at a shop near where she had met the couple — because it looked like the one the little lad had been eating.

It was examined by Spilsbury, who said it was similar in composition to the remains of cake in Willie's stomach. This was a very telling, almost uncanny, corroboration of Mrs Wood's observations.

But something even more dramatic was to come. Asked by a juror in the coroner's court if she had seen the man since, Mrs Wood electrified the court by pointing to Starchfield.

*John Starchfield*

"Yes. There," she said.

Things looked even blacker for Starchfield when another witness identified him in court. This was Richard White, a commercial traveller. He said that just before two o'clock on 8 January, he saw an Italian-looking man with a slightly-built little boy at the booking office at Camden Town station. Pointing to Starchfield, he said: "That is the man."

"It's a damned lie," shouted Starchfield. The jury thought otherwise. He was charged with murder.

His trial opened at the Old Bailey on 31 March. But at the close of the Prosecution evidence the judge directed the jury to acquit him, saying that the case turned entirely on evidence of identification which in itself was not satisfactory. A hero once more, cheered by the crowd as he left the Old Bailey, Starchfield lived for only two more years. He died, as a delayed result of his old bullet wound, in April 1916.

Officially, the murder of little Willie Starchfield remains unsolved. But Chief Inspector William Gough, who handled the case from start to finish, was convinced that he knew the answer to the mystery. Gough believed that Starchfield had intended merely to abduct Willie, in order to cause mental anguish to the boy's mother. Having met the lad in the street, and bought him a cake, he boarded the train with him at about two o'clock. There was an argument, and Starchfield, a vicious-tempered man, struck the boy. Alarmed at his cries, he put a piece of the cord he used to tie up his newspapers round his son's throat "to try to quieten him".

Starchfield's own theory was that associates of Stephen Titus, the mad Armenian whom he had captured, had killed his son out of revenge. The police pooh-poohed this, BUT Starchfield's solicitor *did* find three witnesses who saw, in the vicinity of Willie's home, a boy answering Willie's description being led along by a *woman* — at about 1 p.m. The pair were also seen on a bus that deposited them at Chalk Farm Station.

It was never established whether the murder took place on the train, on a platform, or somewhere outside the railway. Indeed, in all the maze of mystery surrounding the killing of little Willie Starchfield, only one thing seems clear. It is the terrifying Jekyll-and-Hyde quality of the human heart. For there is no doubt that the man or woman who, out of kindness of heart, bought the small, hungry boy a coconut cake, also found, within that same heart, the harsh savagery to choke the life out of a pathetic little waif of the streets.

# The Case
## of
# Patrick Mahon

Edgar Wallace

IT IS a natural thing for the humanitarian to say, of any man convicted of the awful crime of wilful murder, that he could not have been sane when he performed the dreadful act; and when a murder is done in such circumstances and in such an atmosphere as that which marked the destruction of Emily Bealby Kaye, more profoundly does the mind of a balanced man grow bewildered.

Yet all things were possible with Patrick Herbert Mahon, whose form of insanity took the shape of a colossal vanity. Mahon was a man of pleasing address, popular with women and with his fellow men. For all his anti-social acts he was in the way of being a social success in certain circumstances in those circles to which he had the entrée.

He was born in Liverpool; one of a large family of struggling middle-class folk — a boy of some small talent and an assiduous attendant at Sunday school. So he became an office boy, ultimately a junior clerk. He continued to go regularly to church and took a vivid interest in its social affairs. He displayed some prowess in athletics and was particularly fond of football, becoming indeed a prominent member of one of the local church teams. His early mode of life is described as having been a model for all young men.

At school he first met the pretty, dark-haired girl to whom his life was to become so tragically linked. She was two years younger than he, and their school friendship developed into something warmer at a later stage. Indeed, they were both in their teens when he first proposed marriage. There was strong opposition by both families and it was two years after this — in 1910 — that they were married. He was then twenty and the girl eighteen.

Perhaps it was a reckless marriage. But this at least should be said. If any woman could have deflected Mahon from the path that was to lead to the scaffold, it was Mrs Mahon. With singular devotion she held to him through the black and anxious years to the end. Hers is the real tragedy of this story.

Within a year of their marriage he had forged and uttered cheques for £123 on the firm which employed him. With this money he took a girl to the Isle of Man. He was traced, brought back, and bound over. Mrs Mahon forgave him and they left Liverpool to start life anew.

Ultimately he obtained a position with a dairy firm in Wiltshire. There is no doubt that he had a fund of business ability, and this, with an apparent genial vivacity of manner, served him well for a time. He was still a "sportsman", and played football for a local team.

About this time a little girl was born. Hard upon this Mahon was arrested for embezzling £60 from his employers and was sentenced at Dorchester Assizes to twelve months' imprisonment.

Upon his release he is known to have lived for a while in the neighbourhood of Calne, Wiltshire. There was a mysterious epidemic of burglaries in this neighbourhood, and it may or may not have been a coincidence that Mahon suddenly decided to seek other quarters.

He is next heard of at Sunningdale, where he was employed by a dairy. This time there were some love affairs which provoked a little scandal. Again Mahon was thrown out of work. There is a gap here which the imagination may easily fill in. Mahon had become interested in racing, and, when opportunity offered, attended race meetings in many capacities — preferably as a bookmaker's clerk.

However that may be, it fell on a day in the early part of 1916 that a branch of the National Provincial Bank at Sunningdale was entered at night. A servant maid who interrupted the intruder was ferociously attacked with a hammer. When she regained consciousness she found herself in the arms of Mahon who was kissing her. Later Mahon, who had dodged to Wallasey, was arrested and tried at Guildford Assizes for the offence. It was brought plainly home, and after he had been found guilty he made a whining appeal to the judge to be allowed to join the Army. Lord Darling sternly

*Patrick Mahon*

retorted that he was a thorough-paced hypocrite whom the Army could do without, and sentenced him to five years' penal servitude.

That term he served. A boy was born in 1916, but died a year or two later without having seen his father. Mrs Mahon, left to her own resources, with indomitable courage sought a living for her little girl and herself. She obtained a post with Consols Automatic Aerators Ltd, which had a factory at Sunbury. Her efficiency and energy soon attracted the attention of the heads of the firm, and she was promoted to a responsible position.

Mahon came back from prison — full of promises of reform, anxious to be again with his wife. Observe that he always came back — that Mrs Mahon always took him back. Superintendent Carlin of Scotland Yard made a shrewd observation on this trait. "He was keenly disposed to 'philandering' or having 'affairs' with this or that woman casually as they attracted him. But he never, I am convinced, wished to sever his connection with his domestic hearth. He

107

felt in his own mind that the woman he had married was his sheet anchor; that, if he cast off from her, he would be adrift."

They settled down in a flat at Kew, and Mrs Mahon used her influence to procure him a berth as a traveller with her firm. Mahon did well — so well that when in May 1922 the business was put in the hands of a Receiver, he was appointed sales manager.

Now it chanced that the Receiver of the company — a member of a firm of chartered accountants — in the beginning of 1923 engaged as a typist a woman — she can scarcely be described as a girl, since she was then thirty-seven years old — Miss Emily Bealby Kaye.

Miss Kaye had maintained herself by her own efforts for many years. She was a competent, experienced woman, not uncomely, who lived at a bachelor girls' club, and had managed to put by a sum of money, considerable for one in her position. She was not in the least averse from a flirtation with the handsome sales manager, with whom business circumstances now brought her in contact.

The affair developed rapidly. She at least fell violently in love. Mahon may have thought that it would end as other episodes of this kind had before ended for him. But Emily Kaye was not easily discarded. I think we may accept Mahon's own words on this point:

> Just before Christmas, Miss Kaye was dismissed from the office where she was employed, and, as a result, had a lot of time on her hands, and she wished me to see her more frequently, which I was unwilling to do for several reasons. She reproached me on several occasions as being cold, and told me quite plainly that she wished my affection and was determined to win it if possible. I felt sorry for the fact that she had been dismissed and did, as a result, meet her a bit more frequently. I temporized in the hope of gaining time, but from that moment I felt more or less at the mercy of a strong-minded woman, whom, though I liked her in many ways, I did not tremendously care for.

Mahon was embarrassed — perhaps a little scared. But he

*Miss Emily Kaye*

went on, and there were certain dabblings with francs in which he was proved to have had some concern, with Miss Kaye's money. He asserted that some of his own money had been used in these transactions, but there can be no question that the funds were provided by the woman. Miss Kaye was for a short while in employment, but again fell out of work, and some time in February 1924 she probably became aware that she was in a certain condition. Said Mahon:

> She became thoroughly unsettled and begged me to give up everything and go abroad with her.... I plainly told her that I could not agree to such a course. I agreed to consider the matter, however, in the hope of gaining some time, but she suggested I should take a holiday and go away with her for a week or two, and take a bungalow, where we would be alone together, and where she would convince me with her love that I should be perfectly happy with her.

This was the immediate prologue to the tragedy. Miss Kaye was not as some of the other women Mahon had made his playthings. She could not be easily thrown aside.

109

Apart from this episode, Mahon felt the ground solid beneath his feet. His income was more considerable that it had ever been and, added to that of his wife, allowed a very comfortable existence. He was happy in his work; he was popular among his social acquaintances in Richmond and the neighbourhood. He had become secretary of a local bowling club. Save to his wife, his past was utterly unknown. The future looked full of promise. All this would have to be jettisoned, his career, his friends, his home — and he had a sort of attachment to his wife and little girl — if he yielded to Miss Kaye and took to flight with her.

He fought weakly to save himself. Even so, he might have succeeded, had not fate put into the hands of Emily Kaye somewhere about this time a weapon against which he felt impotent. It was the first of a number of strange coincidences with which the case was marked. No reference was made to it at the trial, nor did it leak out in the newspapers.

Emily Kaye was clearing a drawer of some of her belongings. At the bottom of the drawer someone had placed a sheet of newspaper. And as she took it out her eye lighted casually on the name of Patrick Mahon. Thus she read of his trial at Guildford Assizes.

It may be assumed that she used this knowledge in her interviews with Mahon. She pressed the idea of "a love experiment", and he gave way. He engaged a bungalow on the stretch of lonely beach between Eastbourne and Pevensey Bay for two months, using the assumed name of Waller. This bungalow, known indifferently as "Officer's House" and "Langney Bungalow", had formerly been the official residence of the officer in command of a coast-guard station.

This was at the beginning of April 1924. Miss Kaye received the news with some coldness. She had not intended the "experiment" to last longer than a few days. However, she sold out her remaining shares, and went down to stay at Eastbourne by herself while she looked over the place. Mahon was to join her later.

He was very worried. "I felt in myself very depressed and miserable, and did not wish to spend the three or four days together as she desired, but as I had given my word, and as I felt that I could definitely prove ... how foolish the hope was on her part to expect to keep my affection, even could she gain it, I thought I had better go through with it."

Yet the ruling passion was still strong in him. Two days before he was to take possession of the bungalow with Miss Kaye, he met Miss Duncan — a stranger — in the street at Richmond, and although it was a wet night walked with her most of the way to her home in Richmond. He remarked that his married life was a tragedy, and invited her to dine with him on the following Wednesday. The episode gives a clue to the psychology of the man. Murder must have been very close to his mind at that time, and yet he could philander with still another woman.

On 12 April he purchased a saw and knife at a shop in Victoria Street, and travelling down to Eastbourne, met Miss Kaye at the station. They took a cab to the bungalow, and so the "love experiment" started. So far as his home and his firm was concerned, Mahon was supposed to be travelling "on business".

Miss Kaye had set her heart on eloping to South Africa. She had informed her friends that she was engaged — she had shown some of them a ring — and that her fiancé had a good post at the Cape. In a letter written to a friend on 14 April she said that she and "Pat" intended to spend a little time in Paris before going out. This was the last communication that any of her friends or relatives had from her.

On Tuesday, 15 April, the two travelled to London together. Mahon had agreed to apply for a passport, but when they met in the evening to return to Eastbourne, he told her that he had not done so, and did not intend to do so. A quarrel broke out in the train.

If Mahon's story is to be credited, the woman presented him with an ultimatum when they reached the bungalow. She insisted that he should write to friends that he intended going to Paris and thence to South Africa. Mahon refused, and Miss Kaye, in an access of ungovernable fury first threw a coal axe at him, and then attacked him with her bare hands. In the

111

struggle — this is Mahon's version — they fell, and she struck her head on a coal cauldron. A little later he realized that she was dead.

I mention Mahon's explanation, but few people will be found to believe that it was other than a cold-blooded and premeditated murder. Clearly he knew that he would be free the following evening, for he had during the day wired to Miss Duncan, making an appointment.

His story of consternation and horror has a genuine ring. Mahon was a man of temperament and he felt the reaction. He was face to face with the problem that has confronted many murderers — the disposal of the body. And although he seems to have formed his plans beforehand — witness the purchase of the saw and the knife — he had not the nerve to put them into immediate execution. He carried the body to a spare bedroom and covered it with a fur coat.

That night he spent in Eastbourne, and on the next evening he dined in London with Miss Duncan. He remarked that he was staying at a charming bungalow and induced her to agree to pay him a visit two days later — on Good Friday. He confirmed this the following day by a wire from Eastbourne, "Meet train as arranged. Waller," and sent a telegraphic money order for four pounds.

This was on the face of it the act of a lunatic. The body was still at the bungalow. The man was taking a grotesque chance — for what? He himself gave the answer: "The damned place was haunted; I wanted human companionship."

Unquestionably Mahon's nerve was badly shaken, and yet to all outward appearance he gave no sign. Miss Duncan does not appear to have had any suspicion and she went down to Eastbourne on Good Friday afternoon and was met by Mahon and taken to the bungalow. That day before her arrival he had commenced a sinister work, and there was one room that was barred to his visitor. He told her that it contained valuable books.

The next day he left her at Eastbourne and went by himself to Plumpton Races. Here he was noticed by an acquaintance who attached no special significance to the meeting, although it proved to be of vital importance in the chain of circumstance that was to betray the murderer.

Mahon realized by now that the presence of Miss Duncan was going to embarrass him. So he concocted a telegram in a ficititious name and despatched it to himself as Waller at the bungalow, making an appointment in London for an early hour on Tuesday morning. Thus he was afforded an excuse for cutting short Miss Duncan's stay. They returned to town on Easter Monday, and somewhere about midnight Mahon arrived at his home at Kew.

He was back at the bungalow on Tuesday. Here I may tell a curious story which did not come out in evidence. He had already partly dismembered the body, and he now set to work with the intention of disposing of the remains piecemeal. The day was dark and heavy. He built a huge fire in the room and upon this placed the head. At that moment the storm broke with an appalling crash of thunder and a violent flash of lightning. As the head lay upon the coals the dead eyes opened, and Mahon, in his shirtsleeves as he was, fled blindly out to the rainswept shingle of the deserted shore. When he nerved himself to return, the fire had done its work.

It was an extraordinary coincidence that whilst he was giving evidence at his trial a thunderstorm was also raging. He gave calm denial when he was asked if he had desired the death of Miss Kaye. Almost on his words the court was illumined by lightning and re-echoed with the crash of thunder. Mahon shrank into a corner of the dock. Those who saw his face and knew the truth will never forget that moment when the sound of the storm brought back to his mind that fearful midnight scene. He was a broken man when he faced the deadly cross-examination of Sir Henry Curtis Bennett.

Mahon discovered that with every method his ingenuity could suggest the disposal of the body was likely to be a long job. Meanwhile he had to show himself at his office and his home. He returned to his home on the Tuesday night, and during the rest of the week he had to be at his work. On Saturday and Sunday he renewed his labours. On Sunday he conceived the idea of distributing some pieces of the dismembered body from a railway carriage window.

He spent some time over the gruesome business of packing a Gladstone bag. No chance seems to have offered itself on the journey to London that evening but he did succeed in getting rid of some portions between Waterloo station and Richmond. But he was unable completely to empty the bag, and he decided to go on to Reading. The night he spent at an hotel in that town.

The next day — Monday — he returned to London. The bag was now empty save for the wrappings he had used and a cook's knife. These he probably intended to destroy later. He was acute enough to realize that if he had thrown them away they might have been identified.

The bag he left at one of the cloakrooms at Waterloo station and went home. Now, although Mrs Mahon had forgiven more than most women would have done, she was a person of intelligence. Mahon's strange comings and goings of late, his messages by telegram, his stories of business out of town, did not altogether impose on her. She knew him too well. Still, although she could not fail to be suspicious, no glimmer of the dreadful truth was present in her mind. Someone had mentioned casually that he had met Mahon at Plumpton Races and she feared that this was an explanation. Her husband had been previously mixed up with bookmaking and, in spite of his promises to her, it was possible that he had gone back.

By some means she gained possession of the cloak-room ticket. She took a friend into her confidence — he had been formerly connected in some way with the railway police — and asked him to discover what it referred to. She had a belief that it might be some of the paraphernalia used by bookmakers. Thus it came about that the bag was closely examined. It was locked, but by pulling at the ends some indication of its grim secret was revealed.

Scotland Yard was immediately informed, and Chief Detective Inspector Savage had men posted to watch the cloakroom. Mrs Mahon was informed that there was nothing to suggest that her husband was bookmaking.

Mahon returned for the bag on the Friday evening (2 May). As it was handed to him a detective stopped him. "Rubbish," he exclaimed when told that he would be taken to a police station. This little touch of bravado did not help him. He was taken to the station and later to Scotland Yard. The bag was opened and was found to contain a cook's knife which had been recently used, two pieces of silk, a towel, a silk scarf, a pair of torn knickers, and a brown canvas racquet case. Most of these things were bloodstained, and the whole contents of the bag had been heavily sprinkled with a disinfectant.

Savage confronted his prisoner with these things and asked for an explanation. Mahon explained, lamely, that he had carried meat for dogs in the bag. "That will not do," said the Inspector. "These stains are of human blood." "You seem to know all about it," retorted Mahon.

For a quarter of an hour or more there was silence. Then Mahon spoke. "I wonder," he said, "if you can realize how terrible a thing it is for one's body to be active and one's mind to fail to act."

Apart from one other muttered remark, there was again silence for three-quarters of an hour. Mahon came to a resolve. "I suppose you know everything," he said. "I will tell you the truth."

He was cautioned, and then he told for the first time his version of the grim tragedy. I have drawn upon this and his subsequent statements in this account of the affair.

The Scotland Yard experts and the East Sussex Constabulary at once got to work. A search of the bungalow revealed many traces of the crime. There were portions of the body, and evidence of the attempt to get rid of it. But two very important parts of the body were missing. No trace of the head could be found. This, in all probability, would have shown exactly how the murder was committed. There was no trace of the uterus.

The trial opened at Lewes Assizes during July 1924, before Mr Justice Avory, an experienced and strong criminal judge. Sir Henry Curtis Bennett led for the Crown, and Mr J. D. Cassels, K.C., for the defence.

The point taken by the defence was that the death of Miss Kaye was an accident, that either, during a struggle between Mahon and Miss Kaye, she had died from striking her head against a coal cauldron, or that in fighting her off he had unintentionally strangled her. Mr Cassels handled the case with notable skill, but he had to fight some deadly and almost irresistible inferences.

Although Sir Bernard Spilsbury, the eminent pathologist, refused to commit himself to an opinion on the precise manner of death, he was definite in his assertion that it could not have been caused by the woman striking her head against the coal cauldron. He was able to say that Miss Kaye, had she lived, would have become a mother.

All the shifts and deceits of Mahon during his intrigue with Miss Kaye were exposed to the jury. It was shown that over £500 of Miss Kaye's savings had disappeared. Three one hundred pound notes which had been in her possession were shown to have been changed by Mahon in false names at various places. Overwhelming motives were shown by which he might have been actuated to murder.

The judge's charge to the jury was a lucid, perfectly fair, but damning summary of the case. Within three-quarters of an hour afterwards, the jury had found Mahon guilty.

You may say, as has been said, that none but a lunatic could have acted as he did; but apart from the deed, Mahon acted like a sane, calculating man.

I have referred to Mahon's vanity: it is a peculiar trait in all the "great" murderers that they desire to be thought well of. He cannot bear the thought of leaving a stunned servant maid with a bad impression (not unnatural) of the man who assaulted her. He is at all times anxious to be considered by his respectable companions as a man of substance and a prince of good fellows.

There never was a more cold-blooded murderer, except perhaps George Joseph Smith, than this unspeakable villain. Even at the end, when he confessed his guilt to the prison officials, he begged that they would not make public his confession for fear of the "bad impression it might make".

# Murder
# in a
# Trunk

Frederick Porter Wensley

(Ex-Chief Constable, Criminal Investigation Department,
New Scotland Yard)

FEW PEOPLE realize the amount of work that is involved in any complicated murder investigation. Quite apart from all other things, the clerical labour alone is immense. I have known hundreds and even as many as a thousand statements taken in one case. A huge pile of material is accumulated, and, of course, no one knows at the outset what may or may not be irrelevant. There are things that have no seeming importance by themselves till taken in conjunction with other information gathered later. All kinds of people fancy they can provide a clue. This, incidentally, is one of the arguments in favour of a national detective organization. Small police forces have not the machinery to deal with a big inquiry of this nature. They are liable to become snowed under.

How many individuals were seen and statements taken before John Robinson was arrested for the murder of Mrs Minnie Bonati I hesitate to say. There was an enormous amount of good detective work put into the case, but the unravelling of the mystery was due, in a great measure, to appreciation of the significance of such trifles as laundry-marks and a half-burnt matchstick.

On Tuesday, 10 May 1927, Divisional Detective Inspector Steele, of Bow Street, reported that a trunk which had been left in the cloakroom at Charing Cross railway station had been found to contain the dismembered body of a woman. With Superintendent Hawkins I went along to decide what steps should be taken. We felt that this was one of those cases where the murder might have happened anywhere, and Chief Detective Inspector George Cornish was sent from Scotland Yard to handle the investigation.

The details on which he had to work were at first rather misleading than helpful. There was no certainty as to the day or time when the trunk had been deposited, and the condition of the body suggested that the woman had been dead longer

119

than in fact she had. The letter "A" was painted at each end of the trunk, and the initials "I.F.A." were on the lid. A tie-on label was addressed in block letters, "F. Austin to St Lenards [sic]." Among a quantity of bloodstained clothing was an article marked "P. Holt", and another with two laundry marks — one plainly "447," the other with a blurred figure or letter, which might have been either "18 — " or " — 81," but in fact was "581".

One of the earliest steps was to see if there was a Mr F. Austin at St Leonards. A gentleman of this name was traced, but it was quite obvious that he could have had nothing to do with the crime. Meanwhile, the newspapers were supplied with photographs of the trunk, and active direct inquiries made at places where second-hand trunks were sold, and at laundries. Some vehicle must have been used to carry the trunk to the station, and as the most likely probability was a cab, inquiries were also pushed among London taxi drivers.

Within twenty-four hours of the discovery of the crime we had traced the marked clothing as coming from the house of a family named Holt, who lived in Chelsea. One at least of the garments had belonged to a Miss Holt, but she was alive and well. Her mother, however, was able to identify the body as that of a woman who had been in her service as a cook, but had been discharged, after a week, in the previous year. The name she had passed under was "Mrs Roles". Beyond the fact that there existed a Mr Roles, she could tell us little more of importance.

This diverted that portion of the inquiry to the whereabouts of Roles, whose address was unknown. All that night I was out assisting in the direction of the search. By the early morning the man had been traced and was invited to come to the local police station. There, with my old friend the late Superintendent Hawkins and Cornish, I saw him. He was quite frank with us. The woman had used his name but was not his wife. They had lived together for a time, but there had been some amount of bickering, and finally they had parted. His story and that of his employer showed that it would have been utterly impossible for him to have had any concern with the murder.

Through a girl who had known the dead woman, we gathered that her real name was Mrs Minnie Bonati, and that she had been the wife of an Italian waiter. We found this man within a short while. He had been separated from his wife for a considerable period, and it was quickly evident that no suspicion could attach to him. We were now, however, definitely sure of the identity of the dead woman — he had recognized her by a crooked index-finger — and we had gleaned a number of facts about her habits and temperament that might prove useful. The last time she had been seen alive was at about four o'clock on the afternoon of 4 May.

Developments had meanwhile taken place in other directions. A picture of the trunk had been recognized by a dealer in second-hand baggage as having been bought from his shop in the Brixton Road some days before the discovery at the cloakroom. He was quite definite that it was the same trunk, and indeed, the distinctive marks on it left little room for mistake. It had been sold to a man who said that he required some old cheap thing to hold a few clothes and oddments for shipping abroad. There was some haziness about the description of the man, and only very general details of his appearance could be gathered. Another difficulty was that there was some uncertainty as to the actual date on which the purchase took place.

I do not wish the reader to imagine that the sequence of events in the investigation went quite so smoothly as I have set them down. There are many persons who disappear every year for reasons that have nothing to do with crime, and all kinds of people had to be seen before the body was finally identified. Other cross-currents to divert the energies of the detectives arose. For instance, in the course of the inquiries at Hastings and St Leonards, the name "P. Holt" was found in a hotel register. A resident in Brixton came forward with a story of a lodger answering the description (so far as it went) of the man who had bought the trunk and who had vanished at about that time. These things were pure coincidence and had nothing to do with the case. Again, there were men with whom Mrs Bonati was believed to have been associated to be looked for — in particular, a chauffeur with whom she was said to have been very friendly and of whom we knew only the Christian name. All these trails led nowhere.

One little piece of luck had come our way. A boy — a shoeblack — had picked up a piece of crumpled paper that he had noticed blowing about Charing Cross station. Opening it, he found that it was a cloakroom ticket which on examination proved to be the veritable voucher that had been given for the black trunk.

This enabled us to fix the day upon which it had been left as 6 May. The ticket whose number preceded this one had been issued to a woman who remembered, for some special reason, the exact time at which she had arrived at the station in a cab and entrusted her trunk to a porter for deposit in the cloakroom. So we were able to limit our questions to porters on duty at the time. In fact, the same man had dealt with both trunks. The second one — the black trunk — had also been brought by taxi, and he remembered that it had been wedged so tightly on the cab that a little piece of the lid had given way as he tried to extricate it.

Thus we arrived at the practical certainty that the black trunk had been taken to the station by taxicab, and we were clear within a minute or two of the time of arrival. There were, I think, three or four cabmen who informed us that they had driven fares with trunks lettered "A" to and from various places. This was to be expected, for on any given day numbers of people travel by cab in London with trunks carrying their initials. But there was only one cabman who had carried a trunk of this particular description, at about this particular hour, to Charing Cross station on that day.

The method by which we confirmed the time was interesting. This taximan had driven two men who were in a great hurry to get from the vicinity of the Royal Automobile Club to the Westminster Police Court in Rochester Row. Immediately after he had set them down, a man had hailed him from the opposite side of the road. This man had asked the driver to assist him to get a heavy trunk from inside the

*The left luggage cloakroom at Charing Cross station.*

doorway of a block of offices to the cab. The taximan was struck by the weight of the trunk.

"What have you got in here — money?" he asked jocularly.

"No — it's books," replied the other.

He was then driven to Charing Cross station.

Now, it was a pretty safe guess that the men who were in such haste to get to the court were motorists who were due to attend a hearing for some motoring offence. The summonses that had been dealt with that day were looked up. Thus we found two people who were able to fix the time of the incident with pretty close accuracy. Allowing for the time taken by the journey, it corresponded to the time at which the trunk had arrived at Charing Cross station.

All this fitted in with another fact that had been ascertained. The conductor of an omnibus on the route between Brixton and Victoria remembered on 6 May assisting a passenger, who got on the bus in the Brixton Road, to get a large empty trunk aboard. This man had booked to Victoria but had got off somewhere between Vauxhall and Victoria — the conductor could not remember precisely where, as he was collecting fares at the time. Now, Rochester Row is a turning off the bus routes between these points.

We were narrowing down the investigation but were still a long way from the solution of the mystery. Obviously, the key lay somewhere quite close to Rochester Row. There was the block of business offices where the man with the trunk had been picked up, and we turned our attention to these, although we realized the possibility that the trunk might have been brought to that doorway from some other place. Every available person engaged in the offices was interviewed by Cornish, Steele, and other officers. Sure enough, a black trunk had been noticed standing for some little time in one of the corridors, but there was an impression that it had contained books belonging to one of several organizations that shared offices and held periodical meetings on the top floor of the building. There was a little difficulty in tracing all these people. Another set of empty offices bore the inscription "Edwards & Co., Estate & business Transfer Agents".

Who, we asked, were Edwards & Co.? where had they gone?

It appeared that the rooms had been taken by a Mr John Robinson in March. He had started business as Edwards & Co, and on 9 May the landlord had received a letter from him in the following terms: "Dear Sir, — I am sorry to inform you that I have gone broke, so cannot use your office further. Let the people who supplied the typewriter take it away. My rent is paid."

Beyond all question it was necessary to find Robinson. Quite possibly he would prove to have as little to do with the crime as the people we had previously traced — Austin, Roles, Bonati, and others. That remained to be seen. The cheque that he had paid to the landlord led to inquiries at the bank. From that we found that he had been living in lodgings at Camberwell. On 6 May he had left them, saying he was going to Lancashire. Really, he had merely gone to apartments at Kennington, not far away. But in the rooms he had vacated

124

there was a telegram he had sent to a person at a certain address which had been returned to him undelivered. In fact, this was a mistake. The person to whom it had been sent was actually at that place. We kept quiet watch, and when, on the evening of Thursday, 19 May, this individual met Robinson in the street near the Elephant and Castle, two officers were close at hand and invited Robinson to come to Scotland Yard. He readily agreed.

I made a point of being present a part of the time when he was interviewed by Cornish. There was nothing in his appearance or manner to suggest a man who would commit a cold-blooded murder. He had all his wits about him and told his story with great plausibility. He had been all sorts of things. Originally a Blackpool tram conductor, he had served in the army until discharged as medically unfit in 1923. He went to Ireland, where he was "married" — bigamously, as we discovered — and had afterwards stayed in Bradford and Folkestone and London. He had been greengrocer, bookmaker, milkman — but his chief occupation had been that of a public-house barman. Finally, he had started as an estate agent, but had been obliged (so his story went) to close his office for lack of funds. On the day the murder took place — 4 May — he had met a Guards bandsman in a public house, and they had remained there till about three o'clock, when the soldier accompanied Robinson to his office and stayed with him till half-past four. Robinson closed his office about five and went to his lodgings. He remarked, "I don't remember seeing any trunk or bag in the entrance to the office on Friday, 6 May. So far as I know, I have never seen Mrs Bonati or any of her associates."

As it chanced, both the man who had sold the trunk and the cabman who had carried it to Charing Cross station were at this time suffering from illnesses which made it impossible for them to leave their homes. These were the only people who could be expected to remember anything of the appearance of the man with the black trunk. Robinson was asked whether he had any objection to going to them. Quite nonchalantly and cheerfully he expressed his readiness, and his acceptance of this somewhat unusual course was a point in his favour. Both of them, in fact, failed to identify him. It transpired, later, that he had turned down the brim of his hat, pulled up his coat collar and taken other precautions so that he should not be easily recognized again by people who had no special reason to take note of him. The willingness to confront them was an example of brazen nerve which I have not often seen equalled.

So far as he was concerned, there was apparently nothing more to be done. There was no indication that he had been in any way connected with the dead woman or with the trunk. He was allowed to go.

Nine days had passed since the discovery of the body. One avenue after another had been vigorously explored, but all our work had led us to a blank wall. We determined on a fresh scrutiny of the whole of the available data to see whether any new line of inquiry would be suggested, and a conference of all officers who had been engaged in the case took place.

Among many other steps taken was a re-examination of Robinson's former office in Rochester Row. This was entrusted to a couple of enthusiastic and painstaking detective sergeants — Clarke and Burt — who probed into every nook and corner of the two sparsely furnished rooms. There was little probability that they would lay their hands on anything fresh, and there was certainly nothing obvious in the office to provoke suspicion. They, however, took nothing for granted.

Robinson was a great cigarette smoker, as was evident from a waste-paper basket in one room into which, as well as odds and ends of paper, had been thrown a large number of cigarette stumps and burnt matches. Clarke settled down to examine methodically every trifle the basket contained. The cigarette ends and the matches were taken out one by one. At last Clarke was struck by the discoloration of one matchstick. Taking it closer to the light, he came to the conclusion that it had been stained with blood. Here was the first definite suspicion that linked Robinson with the crime. When he had cleaned that office, as he must have done with the most scrupulous care, that matchstick was the one trifle that had escaped his attention. If murderers didn't make these mistakes, detectives would often have a poor time.

Significant though this bloodstained match was, it was quickly reinforced by a discovery that even more directly implicated Robinson with the crime. Among the articles that had been found in the trunk with the body was a dirty and heavily bloodstained check duster. When it was first looked at, it was in such a condition that no distinctive marks could be seen on it. Now, however, it had been cleaned, and a minute examination showed a number of letters in one corner. These were finally deciphered as the word "Greyhound". It was recalled that Robinson had been a barman, and we went to some trouble to find where the duster had come from. We found the Greyhound Hotel from which it had come; we found that the girl whom Robinson had bigamously married had been working there; and one employee was able to say that that particular duster had been in her possession a few weeks before. There could be little doubt that it had been carried home by "Mrs Robinson", and had been taken by Robinson from the rooms they sometimes shared together to his office. At a later date it was identified by a girl whom Robinson had employed as a typist (who, incidentally, had left before the murder) as a duster that had been used in the office.

These developments had taken place on Sunday, 22 May 1927. The next morning when I opened my daily paper, I was confronted with the headlines:

TRUNK CRIME DEAD END
SCOTLAND YARD BAFFLED
300 STATEMENTS TAKEN
AND NO CLUE

As a matter of fact, that very morning Detective Sergeants Clarke and Seymour had, by my instructions, gone to Robinson's lodgings in Kennington, roused him from sleep, and asked him to dress and accompany them to Scotland Yard.

They arrived a little earlier at the Yard than had been expected. After a while Cornish saw Robinson for a moment and told him that he would see him shortly in connection

127

with the statement that he had already made. There was an interval, and Robinson became impatient.

"Will you ask Mr Cornish to see me?" he said. "I want to tell him all about it."

Cornish went in, and Robinson, after the usual warning, plunged into his story. He had, he said, fallen in with a strange woman at Victoria station on 4 May, and she had suggested going back to his office with him. She sat there while he wrote some letters, and then remarked that she was hard up and asked him for a pound. He told her that he would give her nothing. She flew into a rage and became abusive. As she came near his chair, he pushed her away.

"She bent down," said Robinson, "as though to pick up something from the fireplace and came towards me. I hit her on the face with my right hand. I think I hit the left side of her face, but at this time I was also in a temper and I am not certain. She fell backwards; she struck a chair in falling and it fell over. As she fell she sort of sat down and rolled over with her head in the fireplace. I left her there and came out, closing the office door behind me."

Then he went home. Returning to his office the next morning, he was surprised to find her dead. "I was in a hopeless position; I did not know what to do," he said.

There followed the grim details of the purchase of a knife, the cutting-up of the body, and the journey in search of a trunk into which he had packed the remains. In a public house he found a casual acquaintance whom he induced to help him downstairs with the trunk. Afterwards he called a cab and took the trunk to Charing Cross station. Robinson added that he had put the cloakroom ticket in his pocket, but when searching for it to destroy it on his way back to his office, he realized that he had lost it.

The knife he had buried on Clapham Common. He was taken there, and pointed out to Cornish and myself a may tree, white with bloom, underneath which a carving knife was found. It was a queer coincidence that this had been purchased at the very place that had been patronized by Patrick Mahon for a similar purpose.

128

Robinson was charged with murder. The point that was chiefly contested at the trial was whether his story of Minnie Bonati's death was true or false. Put quite shortly, the medical experts for the prosecution said that the bruises found on the dead woman were not explained by Robinson's account. Their theory was that the woman had become unconscious after a struggle and had then been deliberately suffocated by someone who had pressed a cushion or some other soft article over her face. On the other hand, it was argued that Robinson had struck without any intention of killing and that her death was due to accident. Perhaps this latter view might have been accepted by the jury had it not been for Robinson's conduct after the murder. As it was, they found him guilty, and he was hanged.

# A Coincidence

## of

## Corpses

### Jonathan Goodman

If they say that it rains
Or gives rheumatic pains,
   'Tis a Libel. (I'd like to indict one.)
All the world's in surprise
When *any one* dies
   (Unless he prefers it) — at Brighton.

   "Arion", *Blackwood's Magazine*, 1841

Dear Brighton, in our hours of ease,
A certain joy and sure to please,
Why have they spread such tales as these
   About thy smells?

               Anon., *Society*, 1882

BY MIDSUMMER of 1934, that year had the stench of decay about it. It was the sort of year that is remembered for what most people who lived through it would prefer to forget.

In Callander, Ontario, an accident of fertility called the Dionne quins was perverted into a multimillion-dollar industry. Only a day or so after the births on 28 May, while it was still touch-and-go whether any of the babies would survive, the father received an offer for them to appear, a constellation of stars outshining singular freaks of nature, at the Chicago World's Fair; he signed the agreement after consulting the local priest, who gave his advice in return for a commission on the deal. But before long other offers, and more lucrative ones, poured in, giving ample reasons to welsh on the bargain with the Chicago promoters, ample funds to contest their claim. The Dionne Quins (yes, with a capital Q by now) went on to become an advertising symbol, a public relations exercise, a product to boost sales of other products. It never occurred to anyone that they might need protection against anything other than breach of contract.

On the sweltering-hot Sabbath-day of 22 July, John Dillinger — "Public Enemy No. 1" and the first gangster to have a fan-club — was shot to death by an impromptu firing-squad of FBI agents as he left the Biograph Cinema, Chicago, after seeing *Manhattan Melody*, in which a prosecutor (played by William Powell) convicted his friend (Clark Gable) of murder. Following the shooting, the most human gesture was that of a policeman, so delighted to see Dillinger dead that he shook hands with the corpse. Spectators dipped hankies in the blood; some lady onlookers went so far as to kneel and soak the selvedges of their skirts in it. As soon as the inquest was over, a queue-shaped mob surged past the body as it lay in state in a mortuary. A crowd even more dense — five thousand strong, it was reckoned, many carrying picnic-hampers — was locked outside the cemetery (and was drenched but not depleted by a thunderstorm — "God's tears," according to someone who was prevented from attending) while Dillinger's remains were interred. Those remains, for which Dillinger's father had turned down an offer of $10,000, weren't quite complete: during the autopsy — a select, all-ticket affair — a light-fingered person with a quaint taste in mementoes had pocketed the brain.

30 June ended as the Night of the Long Knives: Adolf Hitler, self-styled as "the supreme court of the German nation", organized the massacre of ninety or so people whose political views and morals did not coincide with his own. And on 25 July, over the border in Austria, the Heimwehr Fascists attempted a *coup-d'état*. The timing was awry, though: the Nazis turned up at the Chancellery just after the Cabinet had gone to lunch. Still, Dr Dollfuss was shot as he tried to escape. The Nazis refused to allow anyone out of the building to summon medical help, and the "little Chancellor" bled to death on a red leather couch.

Few people in Great Britain seem to have been specially concerned about the atrocities in Germany and Austria — least of all, Oswald Mosley's black-shirted biff-boys, who were far too busy carrying out atrocities of their own, all in the name of King and Country. On 8 June, members of parliament expressed disquiet at the scenes of well-drilled thuggery they had witnessed at a Nuremburg-style rally at Olympia, the night before, and the Home Secretary recited an assurance that "the situation is under most careful scrutiny". Maybe it was some consolation to victims of blackshirt brutality to know that the Home Office was watching what was happening.

A casual scanning of newspapers of 1934 gives an impression of a year that had more than its fair share of death; but this is probably an optical illusion induced by a large tally of banner-headlined accounts of bizarre deaths and post-mortem occurrences. On a blustery day at the recently-opened Whipsnade Zoo, a man seeking to retrieve his bowler from the lions' den fell on the fatal side of the barrier

... the first man to be hanged in Austria for fifteen years was a half-witted hobo who had set fire to a hayrick ... the wife of the Nepalese Minister to Great Britain having died, she was cremated at an alfresco, coffin-less ceremony at Carshalton, South London ... in America, a resident of the buckeye state of Ohio suffered a slapstick-comedy death by slipping on a banana-skin. And in Brighton — addendum to attractions that were part and parcel of the holiday season — bodies were treated as baggage.

BRIGHTON. County borough, Sussex, 51 miles south of London (3rd-class return rail-fare, 12/10d.); on English Channel; magnificent promenade (3 miles) with two piers; fisheries. Pop. (1933 census) 146,700.

Its fortune founded in the middle of the eighteenth century by Dr Richard Russell of Lewes, who enticed rich sufferers from scrofula (otherwise known as the King's Evil) to bathe in — and even to quaff — the sea-water at Brighthelmstone, a fishing village whose sole claim to fame was as the place where Charles II embarked for France following his defeat at Worcester, Brighton owed much of its subsequent prosperity and growth, and all of its architectural splendour, to the morally insane but aesthetically inclined George, Prince Regent, who was a regular visitor in summers from that of 1783 till that of 1820, shortly before he was crowned King, and in half a dozen summers afterwards. The First Gentleman's influence was at least two-fold: his presence acted as a magnet to others, and aspects of his taste were mimicked in the design of houses and hostelries that were erected to cope with the rush.

In 1934, Brighton was still the most resplendent seaside resort in England, perhaps in Europe. Pebbledashed and Tudorbethan residential nonentities were already blemishing the hem of the town, and office blocks, posing as architecture, degrading the skyline, but these were just first symptoms of a disfiguring rash. The general impression was of the Regency: of bowfronts and balconies, of faded stucco, of snooty squares, terraces and crescents (some of which in propinquitous Hove had conveniences for dogs, few of which took advantage of them).

In this setting — and, by a perverse visual alchemy, seeming to be apt to it — there were all the gaudy trappings of a trippers' town: red-blue-and-predominantly-white seafood stalls, assailing the nostrils with the intermingled scents of vinegar and brine... fortune-tellers' booths, their velveteen-curtained windows patched with pictures of customers as celebrated as Tallulah Bankhead, Isaac Leslie Hore-Belisha (whose lollipop-like beacons appeared on the streets that year) and Amy Johnson... arcades crammed with penny-in-the-slot peepshows and pin-tables... a display of waxwork dummies... hundreds of greasy-spoon cafés ("Thermos Flasks Filled with Pleasure") and near as many pubs... dance-halls... an aquarium... souvenir emporiums that did a roaring trade in miniature-po ashtrays, sticks of rock-candy, boaters with ribbons that extended invitations such as "KISS ME QUICK", and naughty postcards painted by Donald McGill. There was even, on the prom, a store that offered not only Rhinestone jewellery and strings of paste beads but also — unsurprisingly, come to think of it — "Ear Piercing While-U-Wait".

Since the days of the Prince Regent and his *corps-d'amour*, Brighton had enjoyed a reputation as a place where sexual illicitness was allowed, expected, invited even; when the town was mentioned in conversation, a knowing wink was very nearly implicit. "A dirty weekend at Brighton" was a catch-phrase so familiar as to suggest that the town had cornered the market as a venue for sexcapades — that weekends were never at all grubby at resorts like Frinton, Lytham St Anne's and Bognor Regis. As is often the case, with people as well as with places, the reality was less exciting than the reputation.

Brighton had acquired more nicknames over the years than anywhere else in the land. In the decade or so following the Great War, when the race-course and the town were infested by villains, "Doctor Brighton", "London-by-the-Sea", "Old

Ocean's Bauble" and other chamber-of-commerce-nurtured sobriquets were joined by "Soho-on-Sea" and "The Queen of the Slaughtering Places". But the preposterous coincidence of the town's being the scene of three of the five known trunk-crimes in Great Britain made "Torso City" perhaps the most deserved nickname of all.

The first trunk-murder was committed in 1831 by John Holloway, a twenty-six-year-old labourer on the Brighton Chain Pier, who was assisted in his post-executional chores by the fact that his victim, his wife Celia, had stood only four feet three inches tall. His crime was brought home to him at Lewes Assizes on 14 December, and he was hanged two days later.

The next two trunk-murders were London sensations.

In 1905, Arthur Devereux, a chemist's assistant, poisoned his wife and two-year-old twin sons with salts of morphine, and crammed the bodies into a tin trunk fitted with a home-made air-tight cover, which he deposited in a warehouse at Kensal Rise. Three months later, in April, his mother-in-law got permission to have the trunk opened. Arrested in Coventry, Devereux was tried at the Old Bailey in July; the jury rejected his plea of insanity (which was supported by a clergyman who asserted that Devereux was "a little bit off the top"), and he was hanged in August.

The third trunk-employing murderer was John Robinson, an estate agent who in May 1927 did away with an aspiring prostitute called Minnie Bonati in his office facing Rochester Row Police Station, and afterwards dismembered the body, packed the portions in a trunk and deposited the trunk in the left-luggage office at Charing Cross Station. Robinson, who had scattered incriminating evidence as if it were confetti, was, like Devereux, hanged in the month of August and at Pentonville Gaol.

As far as is known, there was a lull of nigh on seven years before Brighton, home of the inaugural trunk-crime, became the main setting for more than one.

17 June 1934, the day when a large amount of the first-discovered body came to light, was a Sunday: a bright,

tranquil day, one of many that summer, with the temperature on the south coast rising into the seventies by early afternoon. In Brighton's railway station, on the brow of Queen's Road, the sunlight, softened by its struggle through the grimy glass of the vaulted canopy, descended in dust-dotted, steam-flecked columns that emphasized the shadows.

Four o'clock; the median of a busy day at the station; a hiatus of calm between the arrival of the last of the special trains that had brought thousands of trippers to the town and the departure of the first of the trains that would take most of them — moist, pink-faced, salty-lipped — away after a Nice Day by the Sea.

It was stuffy in the left-luggage office. Occasionally, the movement of a bus, cab or car in the forecourt of the station would send a breeze scuttling across the linoleum-surfaced counter; but this merely rearranged the stale air. And it certainly had no deodorizing effect on an item of luggage that, at that moment, was being discussed in unflattering terms — and not for the first time — by William Vinnicombe and James Lelliot, the attendants on the two-till-ten shift.

The plywood trunk was brand-new. Its covering of light-brown canvas was clean, unscratched — marred only by the counterfoil of the threepenny ticket, number G.1945, that had been dabbed on the lid when the trunk had been left for safe-keeping eleven days before, on 6 June.

The trunk stood solitary on the stone floor, as if shunned by the pieces of luggage on the tiers of wide, slatted shelves. Actually, it had been left on the floor because of its weight. Harry Rout, the attendant on the other shift who had accepted the trunk, had told Vinnicombe that he remembered saying how heavy it was to the man who had handed it in. The only other thing that Rout had recalled of the transaction was that it had taken place some time between six and seven on the Wednesday evening. In his memory, the depositor of the trunk was faceless, formless; he might, just might, recognize the man if he saw him again — doubtful, though. After all, 6 June was Derby Day, and crowds of racegoers returning from Epsom Downs had combined with the usual early-evening commuter-rush to overcrowd the station.

Now, standing as distant from the trunk as the confines of the left-luggage office would allow, Vinnicombe and Lelliot agreed that the smell from it — which they had first noticed a couple of days before and wrongly attributed to a shoulder of lamb insufficiently wrapped in sheets of the *Brighton Argus* — was growing stronger, more pungent, with every minute that passed. Before long — and in no time at all if the fine weather persisted — the odour would be unbearable.

Something was rotting within the trunk; there was no doubt about that. But what? The smell, as well as being noxious, was unique in their experience. In all probability, both men surmised what was causing the smell. Neither of them, however, was prepared to put the thought into words.

"Whatever is is," William Vinnicombe prevaricated, "it's definitely not lilies of the valley."

The conversation about the trunk drifted on; aimlessly, repetitively, uncertainly. At last — spurred, perhaps, by a specially rich whiff — Vinnicombe decided that enough was enough. Leaving Lelliot to hold the fort and to endure the smell alone, he went in search of a railway policeman.

As it happened, the officer he found was hidden from public gaze, having a chat with the constable of the Brighton police force assigned to uphold law and order in the environs of the terminus. Neither officer was pleased at having his unofficial tea-break interrupted, but when Vinnicombe explained the reason for his own absence from his post, both of them accompanied him back to it. Having sampled what troubled the attendant, they agreed with him — and with the more talkative Lelliot — that the trunk gave cause for suspicion; they only nodded their agreement, then hastened from the left-luggage office and began breathing again. Talking to each other, they concluded that the trunk had to be opened and its contents examined, but that the adding together of their respective years of service did not equal the authority to take on the task. The Brighton policeman "got on the blower" to his station, which was a section of the town hall, and within a few minutes (the town hall being just over a quarter of a mile away, close to the sea) they were joined by Detective-Constable Edward Taylor. The latter, a man of action, borrowed his uniformed colleague's truncheon and used it to prise open the two catch-locks on the side of the trunk. Then he flung back the lid. And then, his need for resuscitation easily over-coming his curiosity, he staggered out on to the concourse. Perhaps it was his imagination, but he was sure that the fumes from the trunk had seeped into his clothing. (Perhaps not imagination at all: even a year later, the trunk, sans contents and having had dozens of drenchings with disinfectant, gave off such a disgusting odour that the spare room at the police station where it was kept was dubbed the "stink-hole".)

Taylor was joined by another detective-constable, Arthur Stacey (whose slight delay is explained by the fact that, having been ordered to proceed to the terminus, he had decided to wait for a tram rather than make himself intolerably sweaty by walking). The two of them dashed into the left-luggage office, stared into the trunk, observed a large brown-paper parcel tied with cord of the type that was used in venetian blinds, scrabbled some of the paper away, sufficient to reveal a female torso, and dashed out again. Having recovered, Stacey telephoned the police station to request — no, to insist upon — the despatch of the head of the CID (never mind if it was his Sunday off) and other senior detectives and an undertaker's shell and canvas screens and the police surgeon and a posse of uniformed constables to what he described as "the scene of the worst crime we've had in donkey's years".

By the time the rush of homeward-bound day-trippers got under way, the left-luggage office was obscured by decorators' sheets; a scribbled notice apologized for the inconvenience of temporary closure. The offensive trunk, contents and all, had been removed to the mortuary. Its floor-space had been scrubbed with boiling water and lysol soap, and half a dozen detectives (known in Brighton as "splits") were perusing the remaining left-luggage for indications of the presence of the limbs and head that had been detached from the torso. No such parts were discovered. (But the search did reveal other human remains. A battered Moses-basket, on the lid of which

# DISCOVERY OF THE DISMEMBERED BODY AT BRIGHTON

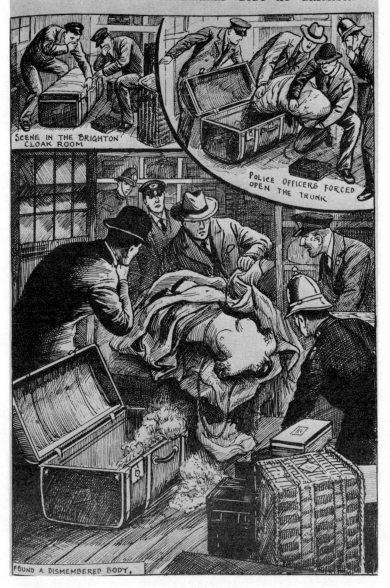

SCENE IN THE BRIGHTON CLOAK ROOM

POLICE OFFICERS FORCED OPEN THE TRUNK

FOUND A DISMEMBERED BODY.

the initials VP had been partly scratched away, was found to contain the body of a baby – a girl who, if she had lived at all, had survived no longer than a few days. As the basket had been deposited as far back as 23 February, Detective-Inspector Arthur Pelling, the officer in charge of the investigation, felt confident in saying that there was "no possible connection between this discovery and the trunk case".) The search was still going on when Captain W.J. Hutchinson, the ex-soldier who was chief-constable of Brighton, got in touch with the duty officer at both Scotland Yard and the London headquarters of the railway police, to ask for all left-luggage offices in the south of England — in coach depots as well as railway stations — to be scoured for suspicious baggage.

At the mortuary, the trunk was unpacked by the police surgeon. Not all at once, but over the next couple of days, the following facts were established apropos of the contents:

Excepting the wounds of decapitation and dismemberment, the torso appeared to be uninjured; a small pimple below the left breast was the sole distinguishing mark.

As well as the brown paper and the venetian-blind cord (19 feet of it; disappointingly unpeculiar, available from thousands of hardware stores at a halfpenny a yard), there were some hanks of cotton wool (used to soak up the blood?) and a once-white face-flannel with a red border. Written in blue pencil on one of the sheets of wrapping paper were letters that looked like f-o-r-d; there seemed to be a preceding letter — *d*, perhaps, or a hasty *l* — but this was only just visible, on the right-hand edge of a patch of congealed blood. Was "ford" the end of a surname? Or of a place name? — Dartford, Guildford, Stafford, for instance. Or was "ford" a misreading? Were the letters actually h-o-v-e? — and, if so, was there a connection with the so-named western continuation of Brighton? (None of those questions would be answered. Towards the end of the week, the sheet of paper would be sent to the government laboratories in Chancery Lane, London, but none of the new-fangled tests, using chemicals and ultra-violet rays, would bring to light the letter or letters that lay beneath the blood; and later, any number of people practising as graphologists would come up with any number of different readings of the visible letters.)

On Monday morning, Inspector Pelling enlisted the help of the press. "What I should like," he said, "is that members of the public, particularly those residing in the Southern Counties, including London, should contact the Chief Constable of Brighton if a female relative or friend disappeared without explanation on or prior to the 6th of this month." (The response to the appeal was over-gratifying: by the beginning of September, twelve thousand letters, cards and telegrams — not to mention many telephone calls — had been received; more flowed in during the autumn and winter, but no one at the police station bothered to count these.)

While Arthur Pelling was talking to reporters — guardedly concerning the crime itself — some of the policemen assigned to the investigation were scanning the Brighton and Hove missing-persons files, others were trying to establish whether those files required deletions or additions, others were at the railway station, working in the left-luggage office or quizzing staff and travellers in the hope of finding people who had been there between six and seven on Derby Day and noticed a man who, perhaps with assistance, was carrying, pushing, pulling or in some less conventional way transporting a trunk.

And at other stations, policemen of other forces were sniffing unclaimed baggage or, more fastidious, standing by or back while left-luggage attendants sniffed on their behalf. One of these stations was, of course, King's Cross, a primary metropolitan terminus of the LNER. There it was, on Monday afternoon, that William Cope, a porter deputizing for an attendant who was on holiday, sniffed and then unhesitatingly opened a cheap brown suitcase. Crammed inside the case were four objects wrapped in brown paper and copies of national newspapers, those wrappings soaked from within by blood and from without by olive oil. Cope looked no further before hailing a constable, who, having taken a fleeting glance at the discovery, blew his whistle to summon other, more senior officers, one of whom felt obliged to pay greater heed to the parcels. Finding that two contained a human leg apiece and that the other two each contained a human foot, he assumed that the feet had been cut from the legs, and that this had been done because, whereas the four parcels fitted snugly inside the case, two larger ones, roughly L-shaped, could not have been accommodated.

The first of those assumptions was confirmed by Sir Bernard Spilsbury, the honorary Home Office pathologist, who, once the legs and feet, still in the case, had been removed to the St Pancras mortuary, went there to examine them. As well as noting that the legs and feet were, so to say, a matching set, he concluded that they had been chopped from the body of a woman — a natural blonde, he believed, basing that opinion on a microscopic examination of the faint down on the legs. The state of the feet — free of corns or other blemishes, the nails expertly trimmed — led Sir Bernard to believe that the woman had worn decent shoes (size $4\frac{1}{2}$, he reckoned) and that she had paid regular visits to a chiropodist, the final visit being shortly before her death.

By the time the police received the pathologist's report, officers at King's Cross had learned that the suitcase had been deposited round about half-past one on the afternoon of 7 June, the day after the trunk was left at Brighton station; they had interviewed Cyril Escott, the attendant who had issued the ticket, but had been unable to jog from him the slightest recollection of the person to whom he had issued it. However, the newspapers that had been used as wrappings — one dated Thursday, 31 May, the other Saturday, 2 June — seemed to provide a small and very general clue: after looking at the blood-and-oil-sodden sheets, a newspaper printer said that the "make-up", and "compositor's dots" on a front page, showed that the papers were copies of editions distributed within about fifty miles of Fleet Street.

Sir Bernard Spilsbury travelled to Brighton to examine the torso. He was occupied for three hours (during which time a crowd gathered outside the mortuary — a few locals, several reporters, and many holidaymakers, including "jazz girls", some conspicuous in beach-pyjamas, some of these and others rendering the hit-song, "It's the cutest little thing, got the cutest little swing — hitchy-koo, hitchy-koo, hitchy-koo", over and over again) and then informed Inspector Pelling that:

> internal examination of the torso had not revealed the cause of death;
> the legs and feet found at King's Cross belonged to the torso;
> the victim had been well-nourished (which, put with the chiropody, suggested to Spilsbury "a middle-class background"); she had been not younger than twenty-one and not older than twenty-eight, had stood about five feet two inches, and had weighed roughly eight and a half stone;
> she was pregnant at the time of her death.

On the Monday afternoon, Brighton's seaward newsboys, standing at corners on the promenade or crunching through the pebbles on the front, had a cry in common:

"Horrible murder in Brighton! Dead body in trunk!"

The cry gave a man known as Toni Mancini the worst shock of his twenty-six years of life. Since the start of the holiday season, he had been employed as a waiter and washer-up at the Skylark Café, which took up one of the man-made caves beneath the promenade, entered from the beach. On this particular day, his attention had been almost wholly directed at the kitchen-sink. Therefore, he had heard nothing of the discovery at the railway station.

"Toni Mancini" was not his real name but just the current favourite among an accumulation of aliases that included Jack Notyre, Luigi Pirelli and Antoni Luigi. He had committed a few petty crimes, but the Italianate aliases, rather than being inventions aimed at misleading the police, were symptoms of his Valentinoesque dream-world; so was the way he smarmed his dark hair diagonally back from a central parting, and so was his attitude towards a string-thin moustache, which was there one week, gone the next. Actually, he was a native of the South London borough of Deptford, where he had been born on 8 January 1908 to an eminently respectable couple — the father a shipping clerk — with a determinedly unforeign surname; the parents had borrowed from the nobility for his Christian name and made the mother's middle name his, thus arriving at Cecil Lois England.

Still, to save confusion, we may as well refer to him as Toni Mancini. He was already calling himself that when, in 1932 or thereabouts, in London, he met up with and soon moved in with a woman sixteen years older than himself. Though her first name was Violet, and despite the fact that she was still married to a man named Saunders, she insisted on being called Violette Kaye, which was the name she had used during an ill-fated career as a dancer in chorus-lines — first, "Miss Watson's Rosebuds"; finally, "The Parisian Pinkies" — at tatty provinicial music-halls. Subsequent to terpischory, she had turned to prositution, and she was well versed in that trade when Mancini joined forces with her, soon to add business to pleasure by appointing himself her pimp. The partners moved from London to Brighton in the spring of 1933. Occasionally, slumps in the never great demand for the forty-one-year-old Violette's services forced Mancini to work; but more often than not he spent afternoons and evenings in dance-halls, usually either Sherry's or Aladdin's Cave, for he was as much a master of the tango and the fox-trot as Violette had ever been mistress of tap and clog-dancing routines. They shared a succession of small flats, the last being in the basement of 44 Park Crescent, almost opposite the Race Hill Inn on the main Lewes Road.

That was their residence on Wednesday, 10 May 1934, when (according to the account given by Mancini a long time afterwards) he finished a stint at the Skylark Café, went home for tea, had a flaming row with Violette, who was the worse for drink or drugs, and, in the heat of the moment, threw a coal-hammer at her — with such unintended accuracy as to kill her. Flummoxed, he left the body lying on the floor, close to the fireplace. When he eventually thought that he must put it out of sight, rigor mortis was complete, which meant that he had the devil's own job fitting it, standing in an upright pose, into a wardrobe (within which, as the rigor wore off, it dropped in fits and starts, making rather alarming noises while Mancini was trying to sleep). To forestall the arrival of Violette's sister, who was looking forward to spending a week in Brighton, sleeping on the Put-U-Up, in the basement flat, he sent her a telegram:

GOING ABROAD      GOOD JOB      SAIL SUNDAY
WILL WRITE      VI

A week or so later, he decided for some reason to move from Park Crescent to the diminutive basement flat at 52 Kemp Street, the southern bit of a dingy thoroughfare that, after being crossed by a main road, became Station Street — so named because its western aspect was the blind side-wall of Brighton's railway terminus.

In preparation for the move, he purchased a black fibre trunk from a dealer in secondhand goods, not haggling at the asking-price of ten shillings. Having stowed his and most of Violette's belongings in cardboard boxes and suitcases, he transferred the corpse from the wardrobe to the trunk, packed the crevices with female garments that remained, scattered a bag of moth-balls over the contorted body, closed and locked the trunk, and threw away the key. As, on his own, he could hardly shove the trunk, let alone lift it, he borrowed a wheelbarrow, then persuaded two acquaintances, a blind piano-accordionist named Johnnie Beaumont and a kitchen porter named Tom Capelem, to help him lug the trunk to the barrow and trundle the barrow to Kemp Street. When Capelem enquired, "What yer got in 'ere — a body?", Mancini replied, with every appearance of nonchalance, "Silver and crockery do weigh surprising heavy, don't they?"

He involved himself in additional expense in the basement flat, for he decided that as he intended to use the trunk as a makeshift seat when he had more than one tea-time guest, he needed to cover it with something: he bought a square of pretty, primrose-patterned American cloth from

147

Woolworth's. Though, as the weeks went by, the trunk became increasingly malodorous and began to leak body fluids, Mancini continued to have visitors. He was fortunate in one respect: the landlady had no sense of smell — and when she commented on the fluids seeping into the floorboards, he told her that they were a unique blend of French polishes, so were enhancing the boards rather than disfiguring them, a reply that pleased her so much that she asked for a quote for spreading the stuff wall-to-wall. On one occasion, a lady guest broke off from munching a muffin to say, "Do excuse my curiosity, but I'm wondering if by any chance you breed rabbits or ... um ... skunks." "That funny smell, you mean?" Mancini asked. "I must apologize for it. And when I have a minute to spare, I'll remove the cause — which (I hesitate to admit this) is an old pair of football boots, reminders of my lost youth: QPR were keen to sign me on, you know. Won't you partake of the raspberry junket? I made it with my own fair hands, and it would be such a shame to let it go off."

When, on the afternoon of Monday, 17 June, Mancini was allowed a five-minute break from his chores in the kitchen of the Skylark Café, he sauntered between the white-painted cast-iron tables and out on to the beach. There he heard the newsboys' cry. Assuming, reasonably enough, that he was the only person in or anywhere near Brighton who had lately put a body in a trunk, he furthermore assumed that Kemp Street was at that moment a hive of police activity; and, once he was able to hear his thoughts above the beating of his heart, he registered surprise, astonishment even, that the only uniformed person within arresting distance of him was a deck-chair attendant. Extending his five-minute break, he staggered across the pebbles to where the occupant of a deck-chair was reading a copy of a special edition of the *Brighton Argus*. Forcing himself to look over the man's shoulder, he read the headlines above, and stared at the picture illustrating, the report of the trunk-crime. Of a trunk-crime that was quite independent of his own. At last believing the unbelievable, he strode back to the café. And he whistled a happy tune.

You will recall that when Toni Mancini first heard of what came to be called "Brighton Trunk-Crime No. 1" — differentiating it from the death and subsequent bundling of Violette Kaye, which was billed as "Brighton Trunk-Crime No. 2" — Sir Bernard Spilsbury was toiling over the torso in the mortuary. Also, policemen were traipsing the town, some checking on whether women reported missing were still astray, others looking in empty premises and even burrowing in rubbish dumps on the offchance of happening on the head and arms to augment the portions found fifty-one miles apart; and, at police headquarters, a trio of detectives was considering the first suggestions from the public regarding the identity of the victim (who, by the way, had already been dubbed "The Girl with the Pretty Feet" by a London crime-reporter — the same man, perhaps, who would call Violette Kaye "The Woman with Dancer's Legs" and her terminal souteneur "The Dancing Waiter"). And, some time during the same period, Captain Hutchinson, the chief constable, had a word with Inspector Pelling and then telephoned the Commissioner of the Metropolitan Police to request that Scotland Yard detectives be sent to Brighton to take control of the investigation; by making the request promptly, Captain Hutchinson ensured that the cost of the secondment would not have to be met by local rate-payers.

The "murder squad" detective chosen for the assignment was Chief Inspector Robert Donaldson, who was, in comparison with most other policemen, quite short. His relative diminutiveness and neat apparel might have led people to believe that he was a "desk-top detective"; also that he lacked endurance. Both notions would have been far from the truth. Not only had he taken part in a number of murder investigations, but on several occasions he had "gone in mob-handed" to arrest violent criminals, some carrying firearms. Any doubts about his stamina would be dispelled by his sojourn in Brighton, during which he worked eighteen hours a day, seven days a week, for months on end.

The detective-sergeant who accompanied Donaldson to Brighton was Edward Sorrell, who at twenty-six had only recently joined Scotland Yard. Donaldson had not worked with him before, but chose him as his assistant after talking to him and getting "an impression (proved accurate) of intelligence and alertness". (That and subsequent otherwise unattributed quotations are from letters that Robert Donaldson wrote to me from his home in New Zealand in the early 1970s.)

Donaldson knew that it was vital to get the support of Arthur Pelling, who might feel put out at having had control of the investigation taken away from him. This he succeeded in doing; indeed, the two men became friends. Donaldson considered Pelling "a very competent detective. A Sussex man whose father had been in the force, he was serious-minded and conscientious. He showed no resentment that Scotland Yard were summoned to the inquiry, and it was largely through his efforts that the Brighton Constabulary, as a whole, were most co-operative."

Captain Hutchingson arranged for Donaldson to have a team of a dozen detectives and uniformed officers, and promised that additional manpower would be provided if and when it was required. As no large offices were available to be turned into "trunk-crime headquarters" at the police station, Captain Hutchinson asked the town clerk if there was space to spare in any council-owned premises, ideally in the centre of Brighton. Thus it was that the investigators took over three apartments adjoining the music salon in the Royal Pavilion, and there, amidst the chinoiserie bequeathed by George IV, and sometimes to the muffled accompaniment of string quartets and of choirs eager with hosannas, got on with the task of trying to identify the Girl with the Pretty Feet, of trying to establish who had gone to such lengths to make that task difficult.

The police did all the things one would suppose they would have done; and many that were out of the ordinary. The investigation, uniquely thorough, comprised a myriad of activities, some of long duration, others of a day or so or a matter of hours. For instance:

As a result of what the press called "the great round-up", 732 missing women were traced. A questionnaire was sent to every hospital and nursing home in the country. Hundreds of general practitioners and midwives were interviewed. At Queen Charlotte's Hospital, London, five thousand women, some from abroad, had received pre-natal advice or treatment between the beginning of February and the end of May; all but fifteen were accounted for.

Statements were made by several residents of Worthing, just along the coast, to the effect that a man who had until recently owned a sea-going vessel had offered them the opportunity of seeing a rather unusual double-bill: first, the murder of a woman, then her dismemberment. The would-be exponent of *grand-guignol* was tracked down, interviewed, and dismissed as being "all mouth and no achievement". Much the same description was applied to the several men and two women who insisted, despite clear evidence to the contrary, that they were the "trunk criminals". Donaldson's men took notes but little notice of what clairvoyants, water-diviners, teacup-readers, numer-ologists, vivid dreamers, and people who had been given ouija-boards for Christmas had to say. (One of the clairvoyants, known to his many fans as Grand Wizard of the Past and Future, told a Brighton detective — and, after being shown out of the Royal Pavilion, a reporter for the *Sunday Dispatch* — that "the trunk criminal is probably called George; he has busy hair, works in a wholesale seed-store, and originally used the brown paper found in the trunk for wrapping up tyres".)

Police throughout the country asked register-office clerks whether in the past few months couples had given notice of marriage but not turned up to complete the transaction. The thought behind this question was that whoever had made the trunk-victim pregnant may have bolstered the conning of the girl with indications of legitimizing intentions.

Of the many people who responded to repeated appeals

that anyone who was at Brighton railway station between six and seven on the evening of Derby Day should come forward, two women and a man, the latter a retired warrant officer of the Royal Engineers, claimed to have seen the — or *a* — trunk being transported towards the left-luggage office. The trouble was that, whereas the women — fellow-Tory-travellers from a garden party at North Lancing — were convinced that they had seen just one man coping with a trunk, the ex-soldier was sure that he had seen two men sharing a similar load. Still, his description of one of the men — "about forty-five, tall, slim, dark, clean-shaven, and quite respectably attired" — came close to the description arrived at (perhaps after much "No, you're wrong, Mabel" — "I'm certain I'm right, Edna" discussion) by the women; and as all three witnesses had been at the station within a period of a few minutes, it was reasonable to hazard a guess — based on the station-master's notes of the actual times that trains had reached Brighton — that if the trunk was brought to the station by rail, its journey was short, probably from the west and no further away than Worthing. An artist was called in to make a portrait from the witnesses' specifications, and copies of this were shown to staff at local stations; but though one or two railwaymen raised hopes by saying that the drawing slightly resembled someone or other who at some time or other had entrained to somewhere or other, the eye-witness evidence led nowhere.

An imperfection was observed in the serration of a piece of brown sticky tape affixed to part of the wrapping that had been round the torso. Therefore, policemen called on every single stationery supplier in London and the Southern Counties, trying — but without success — to find a saw-blade cutter with one tooth blunted in a peculiar way.

So as to check a London suspect's alibi, particles of sand found in his car were compared with samples of sand from near Brighton and from sandy-beached resorts east of Bournemouth and south of Yarmouth. The sand turned out to be unique to Clacton, in Essex — a fact that lent support to his story.

Upon completion of one of the early-begun tasks — the interviewing of residents of Brighton who might help to establish the whereabouts of women who had suddenly become conspicuous by their absence — Donaldson ordered that the interviews be repeated. A roster was prepared, its aim being to ensure that everyone already interviewed was revisited — and by a different officer.

Right at the end of the first sweep, one of Violette Kaye's customers had called at 44 Park Crescent and, having been told by the landlady that "Mr and Mrs Mancini" had gone, she knew not where, reported the prostitute's departure to the police. On Saturday, 14 July, a constable had traced Toni Mancini to the Skylark Café and, not liking the look of him, decided to take him to the Royal Pavilion rather than question him at his place of employment. But after Mancini, ostensibly quite at ease, had said that his "old friend Vi" was trying her luck in France, Germany, or somewhere like that — and that she was forty-two, at least fourteen years senior to the trunk-victim — he was allowed to leave.

But Mancini did not return to the Skylark Café; nor did he go to the house in Kemp Street — the front of which had since the day before been latticed with scaffolding, put there on behalf of a firm of decorators who were to start repointing the brickwork on Sunday. No; he sought out a girl-friend and treated her to a plate of cod and chips at the Aqua Café, which was at Old Steine, near the Palace Pier. He was not his usual cheery self. Ever the perfect gentleman, though, he commented that the girl looked rather nice in her new dress (which was not new at all: once the possession of Violette Kaye, Mancini had presented it to the girl a week or so after Vi's demise, suggesting that it could do with dry-cleaning). The girl was still eating when Mancini abruptly asked for the bill, paid it, left an over-generous tip, and, muttering something that the girl didn't catch, walked out of the café. The waitress scurried across to bag the tip. Lifting the cup of tea that Mancini had barely touched, she pointed out to the girl that he had left her a message, scribbled in blue crayon on the tablecloth: SEE YOU LATER, DUCK.

Mancini was already on his way to the northern outskirts of the town, where he would hitch a ride to London.

On Sunday morning, just as one of Donaldson's team was about to leave the Royal Pavilion to start a round of repeat-interviews, including a second chat with Toni Mancini, at his home this time, a telephone call was received from a foreman-decorator, who insisted that the police come to 52 Kemp Street at once. Why? Well, for the simple reason that he and his mates, repointers all, needed gas-masks against the dreadful smell coursing into the street from the nether regions of the dilapidated house.

The detective with 52 Kemp Street on his list of addresses was told to delay his departure. When he left the Royal Pavilion, he was accompanied by colleagues, one of whom was Detective-Constable Edward Taylor — who, you may recall, was the officer who had opened the stinking trunk at the railway station exactly four weeks before. Arriving outside the house, the detectives at once followed the example of the waiting decorators and turned up their noses; Taylor afterwards expressed mystification that the smell, which must have been polluting the outside air for days, had not offended any of No. 52's neighbours, nor the scaffolders, into complaining about it to a health officer. As there was no reply when the detectives banged on the front door (it turned out that the landlady and her husband — he as senseless of smell as she was — had arranged to be away on holiday while the external decorations were being done), they broke it down.

Having descended the uncarpeted steps to the basement, the detectives first of all flung open the windows, front and back. Then the highest-ranking of them pointed an accusing finger at the black trunk and twitched another finger in Taylor's direction, indicating that he had been selected to open it. The detectives, every one of them, were sure that the trunk contained the missing head and arms. Taylor grabbed a sharpening iron from among the stuff on the draining-board and, his head reeling from a blend of stink and *déjà vu,* prised

# DRAMATIC SCENE AT THE MORTUARY

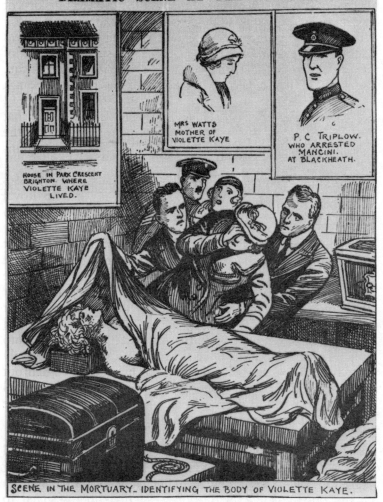

HOUSE IN PARK CRESCENT BRIGHTON, WHERE VIOLETTE KAYE LIVED.

MRS WATTS MOTHER OF VIOLETTE KAYE

P.C. TRIPLOW. WHO ARRESTED MANCINI. AT BLACKHEATH.

SCENE IN THE MORTUARY - IDENTIFYING THE BODY OF VIOLETTE KAYE.

open the locks and pulled back the lid.

You will be aware — basically at least — of what was revealed. Though predictable, mention must be made of the fact that the contents were lavish with maggots, the most gluttonous of which were more than an inch long.

In the afternoon, Sir Bernard Spilsbury visited Brighton for the second time within a month. Following his examination of the body of Violette Kaye, he noted on a case-card that

> she had been five feet two inches in height and well-nourished;
>
> she had used peroxide to turn her brunette hair blonde;
>
> her head was badly bruised, and she had been killed "by a violent blow or blows with a blunt object, e.g. head of hammer, causing a depressed fracture extending down to the base, with a short fissured fracture extending up from its upper edge".

Even before Spilsbury's arrival, Robert Donaldson — depressed that he now had two trunk-crimes to deal with, though "Brighton Trunk-Crime No. 2" seemed to be virtually solved — broadcast a message to all police forces, giving a description of Toni Mancini and asking that he be apprehended.

At about eleven o'clock on the night of Thursday, 18 July, Police Constables William Triplow and Leonard Gourd were sitting in a patrol-car near the Yorkshire Grey pub in Lewisham, South London, close to Mancini's birthplace. All at once, Triplow nudged his partner and pointed through the windshield in the direction of a well-lighted roundabout. A man was walking towards an all-night café. "So what?" Gourd muttered. "Look at his walk," Triplow said. Gourd looked. Yes, there was something odd about it: it was more of a prance than a walk; the feet merely dabbed the ground, making one think of a liberty-horse — a tired liberty-horse. "I reckon it's the Brighton-trunk bloke, the 'dancing waiter'," Triplow said. With that, he left the car and ran towards the man.

"Excuse me, sir," he said, "but do you happen to be Mr

Marconi?"

"Mancini," he was corrected. "I couldn't half go a cup of tea and a sandwich or something."

Triplow and Gourd took Mancini to the local police station. A phone call was made to Scotland Yard, and from there a message was sent to Brighton police headquarters, saying that Mancini would be arriving under escort in the town in the early hours of the morning.

The arrest was front-page news on papers that reached Brighton at about the same time as did Mancini. The reports heaped praise on William Triplow, one going so far as to call him "the sharpest-eyed policeman in the Metropolis". (When I met him at his home in Lewisham in 1970, he had been blind for several years.)

Presently, a queue began to form outside the magistrates' court. Most of the queuers were young women, some of whom bragged of having partnered Toni on the dance-floor, others of whom went farther in boasting of their knowledge of him. Soon there were more than fifty people in the queue. As there were only fifty seats in the gallery of the court, the thousand or so latecomers disorganized themselves into a cheering, singing, waving-to-press-photographers mob. Mounted policemen were needed to bisect it when Mancini, flanked by detectives, made his first public appearance as a celebrity. He looked as if he had been allowed to shave, but his clothes — dark blue jacket, grey shirt, white tie, flannel trousers — were crumpled. He smiled in response to the shouts and screams of "Hello, Toni," "Keep your pecker up," "Don't worry, love, all will be well," and frowned concernedly when a woman in beach-pyjamas fainted, either from sheer emotion or from absence of underwear on a rather chilly morning. The girl he had treated to fish and chips at the Aqua Café stood apart from the mob; she was again wearing the dress he had given her.

Similar scenes were enacted when he left the court, having been remanded in custody, and when, over the next few weeks, he was brought from Lewes Goal, first for further remands, then for the committal proceedings, at the end of

# BRIGHTON TRUNK CRIME NO. 2: SPECIAL SKETCHES

MANCINI. THE PRISONER.

VIOLETTE KAYE. VICTIM OF THE SECOND TRUNK MURDER MYSTERY.

SCENE IN KEMP ST. BRIGHTON—HOUSE WHERE BODY WAS FOUND.

FINDING THE BODY OF VIOLETTE KAYE

ARREST OF MANCINI AT BLACKHEATH.

MANCINI IN THE POLICE CAR. HIS HEAD WAS COVERED

PYJAMA GIRLS FIGHT T° SEE MANCINI OUTSIDE BRIGHTON POLICE COURT which he was ordered to stand trial at the forthcoming Lewes Assizes.

The trial lasted four days. Beforehand — perhaps on his own initiative, perhaps at the suggestion of his counsel, Norman Birkett — he had done some preparation:

"I had carefully rehearsed my lines like an actor. I had practised how I should hold my hands and when I should let the tears run down my cheeks. It might sound cold and calculating, but you have to remember that my life was at stake."

His story — in its essentials, entirely false, as he admitted when the rule against double-jeopardy protected him — was that he had found Violette Kaye lying dead when he returned to the basement flat in Park Crescent on 10 May. As he had a record of convictions for petty crimes (none involving violence — an important point in his favour, Birkett contended), it would not have occurred to him in a month of Sundays to report the matter to the police: "I considered that a man who has been convicted never gets a fair and square deal from the police." So — very silly of him, he now understood — he had bought the trunk, wedged the body in it, and moved, trunk and all, to a different basement.

Birkett brilliantly abetted the lies, saliently by patching together disparate answers from prosecution witnesses so that they seemed to support the theory that Violette Kaye had either taken a mite too much morphine and fallen down the area steps or been pushed down them by a dissatisfied, over-eager or jealous client — and that, whatever had caused the fall, she had struck her head on a projecting rail or a pilaster of masonry.

Holes gaped in both Mancini's story and Birkett's theory: but the jury, having stayed out for some two hours, returned to the bijou court with a verdict of "Not guilty".

Was Mancini surprised? One cannot tell. When he entered the dock to hear the verdict, he was wearing an overcoat — indicating that he expected to walk out into the high street a free man — but when the foreman of the jury spoke two words rather than the fatal one, he staggered and stared, and when he was at last able to speak to his counsel, muttered, "Not guilty, Mr Birkett — not guilty?", as if he were a character in someone else's dream.

(The following summer, Mancini toured fairgrounds with a sideshow featuring a variation on the trick of sawing a woman in half. Instead of a box, he used a large black trunk; his "victim" was his wife, whom he had met at Aladdin's Cave shortly before his flight from Brighton and married a week after his acquittal. He did not draw the crowds for long, and was almost forgotten by 1941, when he was serving in the navy. In that year, a man who really was named Toni Mancini was hanged for a gang-murder in Soho, and people recalled the earlier case, the self-styled Toni Mancini, and said, "Now there's a coincidence.")

While Brighton Trunk-Crime No. 2 had been delighting the populace, Robert Donaldson and his eventually reduced team of helpers had been working hard to solve Trunk-Crime No. 1. Donaldson had reason to believe, but was never able to prove, that one or both of the missing arms had been burned on the Sussex Downs, close to a place where, after the Great War, the bodies of Hindu soldiers who had died in hospitals in or around Brighton were cremated. As to the whereabouts of the head — well, perhaps Donaldson obtained a general indication of its resting place when, early in September, he was put in touch with a young man of the town. The latter stated that "shortly before the discovery at the railway station, he and his girl had been walking along Black Rock, to the east of Brighton. In a rock pool they found a head. It was the head of a young woman. The man explained to his sweetheart that they should leave it alone as it was probably the remains of a suicide and that the police had removed all they needed of the body".

As soon as Donaldson received this information, he caused a search to be made of the whole beach: "Nothing relevant was found, so I consulted various marine authorities on the question of where the head might be; the sweep of the tides indicated that it could have been taken out to sea and then swept ashore at Beachy Head, but nothing was found there

SEYMOURS SURGICAL STORES
(Dept. P.N.) 47, BEDFORD STREET,
STRAND, LONDON, W.C.2.

SEYMOURS SURGICAL STORES
(Dept. P.N.)
47, BEDFORD STREET, STRAND
LONDON, W.C.

# POLICE NEWS

## LAW COURTS
### AND WEEKLY RECORD
THE OLDEST AND BEST POLICE JOURNAL IN THE WORLD,
GREAT GLOVE FIGHTS.

ESTABLISHED 1864

No. 3695 | [REGISTERED AT THE G.P.O. AS A NEWSPAPER] | THURSDAY, DECEMBER 20, 1934 | TWOPENCE

## EMOTIONAL SCENE AFTER ACQUITTAL OF MANCINI

TONI MANCINI.

the trunk

TONI MANCINI RESTORED TO LIBERTY.

MR. BIRKETT

EMBRACED BY HIS MOTHER

SCENE OUTSIDE THE COURT.
MANCINI NOT GUILTY.

MANCINI LEAVING THE COURT, WITH HIS PARENTS

VIOLETTE KAYE
VICTIM OF SECOND TRUNK MYSTERY

either."

The courting couple's silliness was just one thing among many that Donaldson had to hide his anger about. His greatest reason for anger was the action of a high-ranking policeman stationed at Hove.

By early July, Donaldson had garnered indications that the person directly or indirectly responsible for Trunk-Crime No. 1 was Edward Seys Massiah, a man in his mid-fifties who hailed from the West Indian island of Trinidad. One of Massiah's parents had been white, the other black, thus making him a mulatto, his skin dark but not ebony, his hair more wavy than crinkled, his lips quite thin. He had an impressive collection of medical qualifications: MD, MB, B.Ch, DTM. All but the last of those designatory letters, which stood for Doctor of Tropical Medicine, were scratched larger than his name on his brass shingle, which in 1934 gleamed beside the imposing entrance to a slightly less imposing house within sight of the sea at Hove: 8 Brunswick Square.

The fact that he lived as well as practised there was something he stressed in conversation with prospective patients and with gentlemen whose lady-friends were pregnant or at risk of becoming so; he was, so to speak, open all hours, and that convenience was allied with a guarantee of confidentiality. No doubt you will have guessed that he was an abortionist; and it will have occurred to you that abortion was a criminal offence.

Now, a likely cause of the death of the Girl with the Pretty Feet was a mishap during an attempt to abort her embryonic child; if that *was* the cause, then a person who had been involved in the arrangements for the abortion or the person who had tried to perform the operation, or both, would have been most anxious that the transaction and, more important, their roles in it remained secret.

When Robert Donaldson had put together diverse reasons for being suspicious of Edward Massiah (whose qualification of B.Ch was, by the way, a shortened form of the Latin *Baccalaureus Chirurgiae*, meaning Bachelor of Surgery), he found a sum greater than its parts. But as that sum did not equal justification for making an arrest, he came to the obvious conclusion that efforts were needed to ascertain whether there were additional reasons for suspicion — or whether there was a single exculpatory fact. Towards that end, he gathered a number of people together in one of the apartments at the Royal Pavilion; among those present at the meeting were Captain Hutchinson, Inspector Pelling, key-members of the trunk-crime team, and a senior officer from Hove. Donaldson emumerated the points that seemed to tell against Edward Massiah, invited discussion of them, and then — speaking specially to the man from Hove — requested covert collection of information regarding the doctor's background, his present activities and acquaintances, and his movements on Derby Day. He emphasized the word *covert*.

However, that emphasis was overlooked or ignored by the Hove policeman. Having come upon — and kept to himself — a further unflattering fact about Edward Massiah, he went, uninvited and unexpected, to 8 Brunswick Square and laid Donaldson's cards on the consulting-room table. Massiah paid attention, smiling the while, never interrupting. The sun shining through the tall windows glistened on the ranks of surgical instruments, on the green and crystal-clear pots of medication, on the framed diplomas, tinctured the red-plush couch, nestled in the careful creases of the doctor's pearl-grey cravat, black jacket and striped trousers, flashed from the unspatted parts of his patent-leather shoes. Towards the end of the policeman's speech, the doctor took a silver pencil and began jotting on a pad. Notes of what he had said and was saying, the policeman guessed.

But no, he was wrong. When he had quite finished and, pleased with himself, was feeling in a pocket for his own pad — he would need that to record the doctor's exact response — he was nonplussed by what the doctor was doing: carefully tearing the sheets from the pad on the ormolu table, turning them round, and using one manicured finger to prod them towards him. He looked at the writing. Names. Addresses, too. Telephone numbers following some of the addresses. Many of the names he recognized: they belonged to important personages of Sussex, or to national celebrities, members of noble families, or extravagantly wealthy commoners who gave financial support to worthy causes. The doctor explained. These were people who, if he were ever threatened with court proceedings and, in turn, threatened them with publicity relating to services he had rendered them, would do all in their power to protect him and ruin his accuser or accusers. The list of names was only a small sample — come to think of it, he had omitted the name of Lord So-and-So, of the member of parliament for the Such-and-Such constituency, of the owner of the Thingummyjig group of newspapers....

It seemed to the policeman that the sun had gone in: all of a sudden, the consulting room was a place of sombre shadows. The doctor was speaking again — quoting the forewarned-is-forearmed adage, thanking the policeman for revealing each and every fact known to Donaldson, adding that he was much obliged since he could now set about sanitizing most of those facts. And, needless to say, he would make blessed sure that Donaldson — whom he would be delighted to meet some time — made no further headway towards his objective of foisting responsibility for Trunk-Crime No. 1 on a quite innocent person: himself, he meant. Could the officer find his own way out...?

The officer could. And did.

Of course, he didn't volunteer an account of the interview to Robert Donaldson. The latter learnt of the visit from one of the people named by Edward Massiah. The doctor had just happened to mention it — casually, with all the humour of a hyena — to that person, whose consequent fear was manifested as a quietly-spoken threat to Donaldson. The threat didn't worry Donaldson; but the disclosure of the Hove policeman's action made him very angry indeed. Even so, though he got the full story of the interview from the policeman himself, and berated him for "putting ambition before professionalism", he did not instigate disciplinary action.

(Shortly afterwards, Edward Massiah left Hove and started practising in London. There, a woman died following an illegal operation that he had performed. It would be wrong to say that there was a "cover-up", but somehow or other he managed to escape retribution; his name was not erased from the Medical Register. By 1938, he had left England and was living in a fine house, "Montrose", near Port of Spain, Trinidad. Not until December 1952 did the General Medical Council strike his name from the Register, and then only because he had failed to respond to letters.)

At about the time of the Massiah incident, Robert Donaldson brought his family to Brighton: "Not wanting this to be found out by a gossip-columnist, we lived in a private hotel under the name of Williams. I was supposed to be an engineer. My wife and I briefed the children as to their new surname and we thought all would be well. However, my six-year-old younger son, not realizing what was at stake, would solemnly ignore the injunctions of 'Andrew Williams, come here,' etc., and would tell all and sundry that he was a Donaldson. My cover was quickly blown."

Months later, the strain of the inquiry took its toll on Donaldson: "I found that I was having trouble with my eyes. I went to an oculist in London, and after extensive testing he said there was nothing organically wrong with my eyes. He recommended that I see a nerve specialist. His diagnosis was that I had been overworking. Under the circumstances, that was somewhat self-evident. However, I was then given a Detective-Inspector — Taffy Rees — to help me. But Taffy too became a casualty with a stomach ulcer."

There is a final — one could say unforgivable — coincidence to be mentioned. In September 1935, Robert Donaldson took a well-earned holiday. He went motoring in Scotland. On the way home, he parked his car near the border-town of Moffatt and sat on the bridge at Gardenholme Linn for a quiet smoke. Beneath the bridge, tucked well out of sight, were some of the neatly-parcelled remains of Dr Buck Ruxton's common-law wife and of his children's nursemaid, Mary Rogerson. By the time Donaldson reported back to

Scotland Yard, those parcels and others had been discovered, and it goes without saying that it was he who took charge of the London end of the inquiry into the north-country variant on bodies-as-baggage. Though not a superstitious man, he must have been at least slightly worried when he learnt that Dr Ruxton, guilty beyond doubt, was to be defended by Norman Birkett, the barrister who had been so helpful to Toni Mancini. But no: this time Birkett's client was found guilty and was duly hanged.

# Death
## of a
## Countess

Ivan Butler

CONSIDERING THEIR miles of labyrinthine corridors, apparently unpoliced, certainly enclosed, often almost deserted in the very late and early hours, the record of serious crime in London's Underground stations is a fairly good one. But on the night of Friday, 24 May 1957, that record received a horrifying setback.

At about 10.20, Mr Emmanuel Akinyemi, a Nigerian-born lift-attendant at Gloucester Road station, collected the tickets of seventeen passengers off the 10.18 train on the Piccadilly line, closed the doors and started the lift on its upward journey. There was, however, an eighteenth passenger....

Mr Akinyemi delivered his "journey-completed" people into Gloucester Road (almost exactly opposite the house where, in 1945, John George Haigh first practised dissolving his murdered victims in sulphuric acid), collected two passengers, a man of about twenty-seven and a woman in her early twenties, and started on the downward journey. Neither the man nor the woman (who apparently were not together) could afterwards be traced, and of the seventeen disembarked passengers, only four responded to the eventual police appeal to come forward.

Mr Akinyemi opened the doors at the bottom of the shaft, and the two passengers hurried towards the platforms. He then saw an elderly woman, wearing a long black coat and a black straw hat, staggering towards the lift. He thought he heard her gasping something like "Bandits, bandits!" Blood was seeping through her clothing from her chest, which she clutched with one hand; in the other she was holding a handbag. He immediately took the lift to the surface and summoned help. As he did so, the woman lurched across to the ticket office and mumbled some words which the clerk, an immigrant from Poland, did not understand. She was taken by ambulance to St Mary Abbots Hospital, Marloes Road,

Kensington, a policeman by her side. To him she murmured only, "I was stabbed on the platform." By the time the ambulance reached the hospital she was dead — from five knife wounds, two of them in her heart.

She was soon identified as Countess Teresa Lubienska, a well-known member of London's Polish community. She was seventy-three years old, and the hardships she had suffered were appalling. Born on a large estate in Poland, she had married into the aristocracy and had two children, a son and a daughter. In 1918 her husband was killed in her presence — stabbed to death by invading Bolsheviks. She fled to Warsaw and, from nothing, slowly built up a new life for herself and her children by working as an accountant in a savings bank. In 1939, the Nazis invaded Poland, and her son was killed fighting them. She then became involved with the Resistance movement, was trapped by the Germans and sent first to Auschwitz and then to Ravensbrück; somehow she managed to survive in both concentration camps. After the war, following a period of recuperation in Sweden, she came to England; her daughter, an artist, was by this time living in Paris.

By the 1950s, Countess Lubienska was living on National Assistance; her home was a bed-sitter in Cornwall Gardens, Kensington. She was proud of having been elected Honorary Chairman of the London Association of Polish ex-Political Prisoners from German concentration camps.

On the evening of Friday, 24 May 1957, she went to a party given by a member of the association who lived in Florence Road, in the West London borough of Ealing. One of the guests was Monsignor Kryzanowski, a priest at the Brompton Oratory, Knightsbridge, and a friend of the Countess.

At about ten o'clock, they left the party together and took a Piccadilly-line train from Ealing Common, sitting in the seventh, and last, coach. The train was full until it reached Earl's Court, where Monsignor Kryzanowski and most of the other passengers in that coach alighted. At 10.18 the train drew into Gloucester Road station; the Countess left, together with seventeen other passengers. The last coach was at the far end of the platform from the exit, and this meant that the Countess, no longer young and probably tired, walked well behind the others. The train moved on and she was left alone — except for one other person.

According to Dr Donald Teare, the pathologist who performed the post-mortem examination, the wounds in Countess Lubienska's body may have been caused by a large, strong penknife — or, as the police thought possible, a flick-knife. It was considered most likely by Detective Chief Inspector John Du Rose, the Scotland Yard officer who, with Detective Sergeant Edward Greeno, worked on the case, that the crime was committed by one of the "Teddy boys" who at that time were apt to make nuisances of themselves in tube stations: some of them had been seen knocking on the windows of stationary trains to annoy or alarm elderly women.

If one of these youths had taunted or threatened the Countess, she, being both easily riled and courageous, would probably have called him to order in no uncertain terms — one of those terms, it should be noted, being "bandits", which she used indiscriminately to describe ruffians, Nazis, and Communists.

So vicious a killing may seem a disproportionate result of a minor, if nasty, prank — but tempers can flare violently from apparently trivial events; there may even have been an accumulation of frustrated anger unconnected with this particular reprimand from an elderly lady, which caused an ill-controlled youth to "blow his top". One Teddy boy did, in fact, come under suspicion, but was able to prove an alibi.

It was thought that the killer followed her from the platform to the staircase of twenty-six steps that, divided half-way by a small landing, led to the lift, and that there he attacked her, and escaped up the eighty-seven steps of the emergency staircase to the street. There was no ticket-barrier at the end of this staircase, and it was proved by the police that a fit person could have reached the top before the lift arrived. Another possibility is that the murderer stabbed the Countess as she alighted from the train, then boarded it as it moved off. With the remaining passengers and — presumably — the guard in the end coach, this seems unlikely. Equally improbable is the theory that he might have hidden in the tunnel.

There is, however, another alternative, which does not seem to have been considered at the time. The emergency exit stairs are set in a secluded corner, close by but out of sight of the lift shaft. Could the murderer, perhaps travelling on the same train as the Countess, have hurried along the platform and up the stairs ahead of the slow-moving lady who had the entire length of the platform to walk, hidden in that deserted corner, and seized the opportunity to kill her as she waited for the lift's return? It would have been far safer than attacking her on the platform, which has the opposite platform running parallel and connected to it by several openings.

*Against* this theory is the policeman's statement that she said to him in the ambulance, "I was stabbed on the platform," but an elderly foreign woman in her confused state might well have called that part of the station at the bottom of the lift-shaft a "platform". *For* the theory is the doubt as to whether she could have staggered along the platform and up twenty-six steps with five stab wounds, two in her heart.

As for the motive, it could have been robbery (thwarted by the Countess's tight hold on her handbag); it could have been rage at being rebuked for bad behaviour (which might account for the several stab wounds); it could have been just a senseless act of violence. But there was a more dramatic theory — strongly held in some quarters — that the murder was politically motivated.

Among Countess Lubienska's duties as head of the London Association of Polish ex-Political Prisoners was the vetting of claims for compensation for their ordeal in concentration camps. The association was strongly against the new regime in Poland, which kept a close watch on such "dissident" organizations. The Countess may have become suspicious that a Communist had infiltrated the membership; and the latter, in turn, may have realized that he was suspected by her. Such a person would in all probability have known about the Countess's movements that night; may even have been at the party. Steps could have been taken to prevent her from exposing him. Mr Fenton Bresler, who wrote an article on the case in the *Sunday Express* of 17 March 1974, puts forward an interesting point in support of this notion. He discovered that a Polish word, *bandyci*, pronounced "bandichee", means "someone who kills intentionally". Could this have been what the dying woman cried out — easily mistaken by the Nigerian-born lift-attendant for "bandits"?

On Saturday, 1 June, after a period of lying-in-state, a requiem mass was held for Countess Teresa Lubienska at the Brompton Oratory, during which General Anders, head of the Free Poles in Exile, placed on her coffin the high Polish honour of the Golden Cross of Merit with Swords — awarded in this instance, said the general, for "work in the Resistance".

On 20 August, at a resumed inquest, the final verdict was recorded: *Murder by some person or persons unknown.* Thus the English legal decision was laid down. It seems, however, that some Polish expatriates regarded the last word of the verdict with a certain scepticism.

# Acknowledgements and Sources

In addition to those given in the Introduction, MONTAGU
WILLIAMS, QC: extract from *Leaves of a Life*, Macmillan, 1890.
H.L. ADAM: extract from *Murder by Persons Unknown*, Collins,
1931. Canon J.A.R. BROOKES: extract from *Murder in Fact
and Fiction*, Hurst & Blackett, 1925. RICHARD WHIT-
TINGTON-EGAN's essay is published by permission of the
author. EDGAR WALLACE: Introduction to *The Trial of Patrick
Mahon*, Bles, 1927. JONATHAN GOODMAN's essay is
published by permission of the author. IVAN BUTLER's essay is
published by permission of the author.